Statham Island

By

Anita Giannantonio

Contents

Chapter One

It was a warm spring morning as Annette Jameson ascended the steps of her friend's Upper Manhattan apartment. She had been building up the visit for some time in her mind now. She was eager to visit her long-time friend, Christina, but also to discuss a new and important development in her own life. She had told the office that she had a doctor's appointment, an inconspicuous excuse for leaving in the middle of the day and possibly not returning until the next.

She resembled the quintessential New Yorker, and after fifteen years of living in the city, her country upbringing had long since faded. What remained was a polished example of what one can become in the right atmosphere. Her shoulder-length hair was pulled neatly into an updo. Her soft brown eyes hid behind the rims of black frames, which made her appear somewhat older than thirty-five but also gave the appearance of intelligence, which she found helpful in her career as a legal assistant for Brown & Martin, a medical malpractice law firm in town. Her white blouse sat tucked neatly into a black, tweed skirt, impeccably complementing the shiny black heels she had chosen from her closet that morning. A gray and white checkered Louis Vuitton handbag hung unapologetically from her arm. The affluence of the area allowed her to feel comfortable sporting her best accessories.

A balding man in his mid-sixties and wearing a security guard uniform stood outside the front entrance. It was a face she recognized, and over the course of her frequent visits, the two had created a unique bond and looked forward to each other's company. "Hi, Pete!" Annette called out excitedly as she was greeted with a kind smile. He reminded her of her own father, about the same age, and with an equally kind personality. Even though it had been eight years since he passed away, the reminder of the lost relationship always brought her a twinge of sadness.

"Annette! How've you been? How's Mable?" he asked, referring to her golden retriever. Before she could answer, he added, "Christina just popped out for a second but asked me to tell you to wait and that she'd be right back."

The two chatted for ten minutes before a thin, young blonde appeared from around the corner and walked up to the pair, her disheveled appearance catching Annette off guard and making her look out of place on Washington Street. Her hair, pulled into a messy bun, revealed several inches of brown roots; she simply had not had the motivation recently to visit the salon. Her worn and dirty T-shirt, inadvertently left behind by her estranged husband after he moved out, hung loosely from her torso. Annette recognized the faded jeans with holes in the knees and covered in paint splatter as the ones Christina wore for home improvement projects.

It was difficult to believe that this was the same woman who, until recently, was partner at Brown & Martin. Years before, she had left the field of nursing to attend law school and had quickly become a well-known and respected medical malpractice attorney in New York.

While she was known for her mental prowess and breadth of knowledge, she also had a reputation for dressing to the nines eighty hours per week and, as gossip around the office would have it, looked like she had just stepped out of a Vogue photo shoot. As the wife of a commercial pilot and the mother of two children, her life was the envy of many. Until one day when it all came crashing down around her. The person left seemed a fragile shell of the accomplished woman well-known in the community. And it was moments like this that both Annette and Pete realized just how much Christina needed whatever they had to offer…a smile, a hand with the groceries, a funny story…to ease the pain of what she was going through. Pete had become accustomed to assisting Christina and never once accepted a tip, for he hoped that someone would treat his own daughter with the same dignity and respect should she, God forbid, ever encounter a similar fate.

Christina Martin seemed to notice nothing of the concerned look of her friends. She was tired, and a bulky fruit tart was growing heavy in her arms. She invited Pete to join them for coffee, but he politely declined, as his shift ran until three o'clock. Lately, she had seemingly forgotten that other people had jobs to do. It had been several months since she had taken her leave of absence, and having to work was starting to seem foreign to her. While the hustle and bustle continued for everyone else, her life stood still. She and Annette made their way up the white brick, early-nineteenth-century apartment building to the third floor, while Pete went back to greeting and holding the door for tenants. The black and white tiled floor of the lobby appeared to be the original floor and in good condition, too. And the building, despite its old, slightly musty smell, was painted in light colors and had a welcoming feel.

But the cheerful ambience of the building stopped at Christina's door. It had only been two weeks since Annette had last visited, but the apartment looked as though it had been neglected for months. Unfolded laundry sat in baskets in the den; papers, presumably related to the ongoing divorce, scattered the kitchen table; several empty wine bottles littered the floor; and a pizza box from the night before sat precariously on the coffee table edge, its lid open, revealing two leftover slices.

Annette tried to conceal her shock at the appearance of the once-tidy living quarters. But looking around, she wondered whether she had made the right choice in stopping by…and whether

Christina was the right person to ask an important favor of at the moment.

"I'm sorry about the mess. The kids and I were up late last night and overslept this morning. They just barely caught the bus!" She grabbed the pizza box hastily as she made her way to the coffee machine. "How have you been?"

"How have *you* been?" Annette repeated back, knowing that her ordinary routine with occasional work drama was nothing in comparison to what Christina's life had become. She also secretly wanted the latest scoop on the divorce and John's new partner, Rachel. "You look awful," she said honestly. Christina was not surprised when she said it. She had put self-care on the backburner as she struggled to adapt to single motherhood, while maintaining some semblance of normalcy for her six-year-old twins, Charlie and Chelsea. But nothing seemed normal for anyone. Her life was literally in shambles, and the person she had been until a few months prior seemed like a stranger in another life.

"Thanks!" she replied sarcastically, handing Annette her coffee and fruit tart. "You know, things are going. We're getting by, and the kids...well, they're doing the best they can. Chelsea's kindergarten teacher told me that she keeps asking when her dad is going to live with us again." It was clear to Annette that this, in particular, pulled on her heartstrings. "It's just difficult to tell them what is going on without divulging more than they need to know. I hate John for what he's done, but they still need that relationship, and I don't want to be the one to ruin it. I'm sure he'll accomplish that on his own," she said with a little laugh.

Annette was amazed by her strength and was not sure she could be as compassionate if the shoes had been reversed.

"He called me last night. Honestly, I think the guilt is getting to him, and once again, he tried to make it seem like the affair was my fault. Can you believe that? Like working long hours and trying to make the best opportunities for our family was an excuse to do what he did." But even as she said it, she wondered if John was right. Perhaps her busy work schedule and focus on success had driven him away.

"Jeez. I'm sorry. How can you possibly respond to something like that? So ridiculous. I hope you hung up on him."

"I wanted to. But then he told me that she's pregnant. And they're apparently engaged."

"You're kidding." Annette had expected a little drama but nothing of this magnitude.

Tears welled up in Christina's eyes and ran down her cheeks, which flushed as they always did when she was emotional. There was no more holding it in. "He and Rachel have only been together a few months, at least, that's all I am aware of." Annette grabbed tissues from a chair and handed them over, rubbing her back as she sobbed. She had been there for Christina when she and John were going through IVF. She had even thrown their baby shower once the twins came along. It seemed odd to think that John was now having a baby so easily with another woman. Furthermore, it seemed like Christina's hopes and dreams of expanding her family had been stolen right from under her. The two had restarted the IVF process the past December, and at the time, both seemed so hopeful that they would have the same success as before. "I mean shit; my life is falling apart."

"I'm so sorry. You cannot blame yourself," Annette said, on the verge of crying herself. Although she had never been the type to want a family of her own, she considered herself an aunt to the twins. She understood what motherhood meant to her friend and felt empathy for her situation. The two women embraced for some time before Christina was able to regain enough composure to drink her cup of coffee. She no longer felt hungry enough for the fruit tart. The stress she had been under these past few months had taken a serious toll on her eating habits, and she found herself subsiding on nibbles here and there of sweets and fast food. The ten-pound weight loss was visible by the bagginess of her clothes. "He's an absolute jerk and doesn't know what he's losing." And she meant it. There was nobody like Christina, absolutely no other person who had her smarts, her strength, her ambitions, all while being a super mom. She was truly special. And Annette knew that whatever John felt for Rachel would ultimately pale in comparison to the life he had made with Christina.

Between sips of coffee, they discussed the impending divorce a little longer and then Annette's recent trip to Italy and Greece. Before long, it was early afternoon, yet something important remained on Annette's mind. "Would you be interested in helping me with a project?" Immediately, she regretted having asked. It was not the right time, she thought. But then again, maybe it was perfect timing. And she needed someone with Christina's expertise to handle it.

"Project?" Christina responded, feeling slightly annoyed that Annette would ask her for a favor when it was clear that her life was crumbling around her. But she knew that their friendship thrived because they were always there for each other, even when not convenient. "I would be happy to," she mustered. "What are you working on? Did you get another crazy idea off HGTV?" she teased.

Annette had to laugh. "Actually, no. Not this time, at least." She hesitated. It occurred to her that she was indeed there to ask a favor, just not the type one might expect. It had weighed heavily on her mind for some time now. It was an opportunity, she reminded herself, and a mutually beneficial one at that. "Do you remember me telling you about the manor my Uncle Bob was renovating?"

She nodded. Annette's uncle had recently passed away from a heart attack…or at least that is what she heard through the grapevine. She remembered Annette coming into her office just before her own departure, informing her that she would be taking time off of work to manage his estate. She had been devastated, as they were the only two members left in her small family. The two had been very close, staying in frequent contact even though he lived several hours away. Christina suddenly realized, mortified, that she had not bothered to ask Annette how *she* had been in quite some time. The past few months had been a constant focus on her.

Annette went on, "The real estate group has been unable to sell it because it needs updating…mostly aesthetic changes. He was able to do some projects here and there but, honestly, didn't get too far with it. It's got some peeling wallpaper, a leak or two in the roof, a dirty pool, and an overgrown garden. But the realtor assured me that with a little TLC, the property will sell."

Christina looked intrigued, especially since the two shared a love for renovating their own homes, but wondered what any of this had to do with her. Annette's uncle had retired from the police force a decade prior and spent his sixties purchasing properties that he rented out or flipped and resold. It was a hobby that had become a good source of revenue in his retirement. She remembered Annette speaking of the manor that sat on a twenty-two-acre island off East Hampton and the plans her uncle had to open a bed and breakfast once it was done.

Annette hesitated briefly, finally gathering up the courage to ask. "Would you like to do something different for a while? Get your mind off of what's been going on? You could oversee the renovations of the property and stay at the manor if you'd like. I trust you more than any contractor to make sure things get done."

Christina laughed, thinking she was joking. "Are you serious? I mean, I don't feel very qualified. What do you mean exactly? Like, live there while contractors are renovating the house? Or renovate myself?" She quickly began to picture herself trying to fix up an old manor and not just paint a wall but really fix a problem. She imagined the sort of damage she could cause and shared that thought with Annette, giggling as she described falling walls and nothing but a fireplace left when she was done.

"You could help…not help…whatever you felt like doing. You could sit on a private beach all day drinking wine…as long as you make sure that the workers show up and stay on track." She paused. "It's really for you. I want to give you the chance to take a break for a little while. Take a step back from the divorce and work, and just find yourself again. I want you to be happy. This," she said, gesturing towards the piles of laundry and leftover food, "does not look like the sort of place where a happy person lives. I want more for you, and I think Statham Manor would be a perfect excuse for you to have a once-in-a-lifetime, therapeutic break from reality for a few months. Uncle Bob left me with a good sum of money and the properties, and I am happy to pay your price. A good overseer on these sorts of projects is invaluable," she said with a knowing tone, "and I simply don't have the patience or desire to do it myself. Please…please," she begged. "At least, think it over. You don't have to tell me right away. And if you like, I can take you there before you make any big decisions."

"Okay, okay. I'll think it over. But that's all I can promise for now."

Thoughts of the possibilities began to flood her mind, and then, the logistics. How would the kids get to school? Would they be stuck on the island all the time? And was she ever going back to the firm?

Just then, Christina jumped up. "Oh my gosh! I'm going to be late," she shrieked, realizing that it was Wednesday. School got out one hour early each Wednesday, which meant that she had five minutes to make the twenty-minute drive to pick up her children. "I've got to pick up the kids." She almost tripped over her laundry, trying to grab her things as she prepared to leave. Annette gave a quick hug goodbye as she was shoved out the door and thanked for stopping by. She had wanted to tell Christina so much more about the property, but it would have to wait until another day.

John Martin busily unloaded his suitcase in the upstairs bedroom of his Manhattan townhouse. He had just returned from a trip to the Netherlands and was exhausted. This was his last trip for the month and the start of a two-week vacation. As a commercial pilot, he had spent the past fifteen years flying around the world and enjoyed his career thoroughly. But on this last trip, he found himself feeling more homesick than he was used to and opted for an earlier flight home than originally planned. He kicked off his shoes and laid out his uniform on the bed before slipping into sweatpants and a T-shirt and heading down to the kitchen. On his way down, he quickly glanced in a hall mirror. Despite the long trip, his brown hair still sat nicely slicked back with the gel he had taken from the Amsterdam hotel. He examined his stubble and decided to leave it for the moment because Rachel liked it. He straightened out his tall frame, cracking his back, and made his way downstairs.

Rachel Harper had been outside gardening when he returned and ran into the powder room to freshen up before she encountered him. She wiped a streak of dirt off of her cheek and fixed her messy, brunette bun, pulling hair that had fallen back into the hair band. Though their relationship had progressed quickly, it was, in reality, still in its infancy, and she felt a certain pressure to impress.

John saw the powder room light on and peeked around the corner. "Hey, Rach," he said, embracing her. "What smells so delicious?" The smell of something cooking had greeted him at the door. Rachel was a talented cook, unlike Christina, who he like to joke was skilled in the art of burning food. He enjoyed the wonderful, home-style meals that Rachel made and wondered whether he would be eating pad thai, eggplant parmesan, chicken scallion dumplings, or beef bourguignon for dinner, perhaps with homemade cheesecake for dessert. He had gained seven pounds since they had moved in together and reminded himself that he would need to stick to his daily runs on the days he was off.

"Just a little pot roast and a cherry pie," she said proudly, brushing past him to pull the biscuits from the oven. She had always loved being in the kitchen, ever since she was a little girl cooking with her own mother. It made her happy to express that creative side of herself. And now that she was taking a hiatus from her flight attendant career, she found herself cooking…and eating…more than ever. But with a baby on the way, she was not worried about weight gain for the moment and planned to jump back into her workouts and healthy eating routines right after the birth.

The two had only lived in the townhouse for three months. John had not been prepared to move in together so suddenly but had found himself in quite the predicament when Christina confronted him about his affair. He had just returned from a trip and was surprised to find his spare bags, usually kept stored away in their closet, packed for him and waiting by the front door. He was equally surprised to find Christina home from work and looking disheveled. Mascara was smudged under her eyes, and she was wearing pajamas in the middle of the day. Was she sick? Perhaps she had caught the flu that was going around. It had been particularly bad this year. But why the bags? And then the realization that *she knew* hit him like a ton of bricks. For a while, he had promised himself that he would end the affair and believed that as long as Christina did not know, life could continue on as normal. But as much as he wanted to stop seeing Rachel, he found that he just could not pull himself away. He was in love with her. He had wanted to tell Christina that he was not happy in their marriage, but his cowardice prevented him from admitting to her that he had taken their hopes and dreams for the future and squashed them. He had quickly found himself deep in the sinking sand of an affair that he did not intend to go so far, with no way out except the long and painful route that he had hoped desperately to avoid.

"How could you!" she screamed at the top of her lungs. "How *dare* you. I trusted you. I loved you. I gave you two children, you fucking asshole! And we were trying to have another." What followed was a wail he only remembered his mother making after learning of his father's death, only this time it emerged from Christina's throat. It reminded him of how a wild animal in distress might sound. "How long have you been lying to me? How could you do this to me…to Charlie and Chelsea?" She was shaking with anger, and fresh tears ran down her face. She had not prepared what she was going to say to John…her emotions, still so raw, bubbled over into every word she yelled. It was unlike her to cuss, a trait she had sworn away from after the twins were born lest they ever overhear and repeat that type of language. But they were at school, and at the moment, swearing was the least of her concerns. The gloves were off. She happened to be holding a box of tissues at the time and threw it in John's direction.

He ducked and grew angry at her apparent inability to admit that their marriage had been deteriorating for some time. "Maybe if you had your priorities straight, this wouldn't have happened."

"*My* priorities?" she repeated, laughing as she said it. Oh, the irony.

"For years, you have chosen your clients over me. You put me last every single time. We spend no time together unless we're sitting together in the waiting room of the fertility clinic. What kind of marriage is that?" Bringing his voice down, he continued matter-of-factly, "It's just not how I want to live anymore." It was the first time he was able to admit it to himself. He wanted so badly to have been a husband he could be proud of but found it impossible with Christina. How can you possibly be close to someone when your schedules leave you passing like ships in the night? And despite their mutual desire for another child, the financial and mental strain of infertility treatments had ultimately been the straw that broke the camel's back.

His defensiveness only infuriated her further. "So you think this is my fault? I'm not the one traveling around the world with Rachel instead of being home with our children." Saying the name suddenly made her feel ill, and she suddenly wished she didn't know it. "When was the last time you did anything with Charlie and Chelsea? I do everything around here. *I* am the one taking them to school and picking them up. *I* am the one putting them down at night. *I* am the one taking them to birthday parties and on field trips. And I certainly was not the one sleeping around. Get your own priorities straight. Better yet, get out! Just leave! Go home to your girlfriend," she said disdainfully, not truly expecting that he would actually do just that. But John quietly grabbed his bags and left, closing the door behind him, quietly enough to not disturb the neighbors.

Somehow, she hoped this all was a bad dream or, at the very least, a big misunderstanding, but two weeks later, John and Rachel were moving into a rented townhouse together with only Rachel's bed and a small couch, the sole items left after her own recent breakup. The new home was an upgrade for both of them, despite the lack of furniture, and it was the first time in years either had a garden.

At twenty-eight years old, Rachel was eager to settle down. She was not married to her work and freely gave it up shortly after moving in with John. She much preferred to have a free schedule with plenty of time to meet friends and manage the home. And in just six months, she was going to be a mother, a role she had always yearned for.

The two had met four years prior on a flight to Stockholm and often flew the same routes. They enjoyed each other's company, and John found it easy to talk to her. She was eager to listen to his travel stories, unlike Christina, who had grown bored of them, and enjoyed sharing travel stories of her own. Before long, they had skied together in the Swiss Alps, scuba-dived around the Great Barrier Reef, swam in the Dead Sea, visited ancient Mayan ruins, and sailed along the coast of Bermuda, all while on layovers. Rachel was well aware that John was married with a family, and at the time, she had had a boyfriend of her own. Neither had expected the relationship to develop but found themselves growing closer and closer during their overseas travels. Their love for visiting new countries and cultures forged a bond that neither had with their respective partners.

Rachel and her boyfriend broke up early on as he grew uncomfortable with Rachel and John's friendship. He was very quick to notice John's frequent calls and the fact that her travel pictures often contained John, too. But John became very reluctant to admit to Christina that he had betrayed her, even as they continued to go through IVF, which became a heated point of contention between him and Rachel. His hesitance was also rooted in fear of divorcing one of the city's top attorneys, who had greater legal knowledge and resources than any attorney he could possibly hire. Divorcing Christina came with the real possibility of losing everything…his money, his children, and his reputation…in the process. If not for being confronted with his literal and figurative baggage at the entryway of his home, he likely would have never revealed anything to Christina.

But his lack of action had just delayed the inevitable. Quickly thereafter, he and Christina began divorce proceedings. For the moment, she had custody of the twins during the week and he on weekends, although he found himself asking Christina more and more often to keep the kids during his visits. He was not ready to give up his freedom to travel at will or to just spend the day alone with Rachel. And his relationship with Charlie, in particular, was strained at the moment. Visits were becoming more seldom, although he still made it a point to call them a few nights a week. Rachel had only met the children twice and was glad that her focus could be elsewhere instead of on entertaining two kindergarteners.

The two ate dinner and dessert and enjoyed a bottle of sparkling cider that Rachel had picked up as an alternative to wine while John excitedly told her about the drama of his most recent flight. She was thoroughly entertained when he described an unruly, drunk passenger who sang the National Anthem the last four hours of the flight. And she laughed hysterically when he mentioned that he tripped on his way out of the cockpit, much to the delight of a de-boarding child who thought the lanky, clumsy man falling before him was Blippi, a kids' TV show character, there to greet him at the gate. Rachel asked all the right questions and validated his jokes, and John felt truly satisfied with his life for the first time in years.

Christina was exhausted from the day and settled for a relaxing bubble bath as soon as the children were asleep, going to bed herself shortly thereafter. Later that night, she awoke in a cold sweat and physically shaking from a vivid nightmare that shook her to her core. The dream had begun quite innocently in a beautiful garden, maybe a park. She walked the grounds, enjoying the smell of roses and the sounds of birds chirping, when suddenly, the roses faded and withered, crumbling to the ground as if winter had arrived. The air grew cold around her. The sun hid behind the clouds. The birds went silent. In fact, there was no sound at all, not even the sound of leaves rustling as the wind picked up. She found herself nearly paralyzed by an overwhelming sense of danger and the feeling of being watched by something, or someone, unseen. And then it moved. Out of the corner of her eye, something shifted along the tree line…a shadowy, almost humanly figure. It disappeared, then reappeared, from sight, and she felt it all around her. An unnatural laugh echoed so loud that the ground vibrated. She broke into a run but could not seem to escape it. Every leap felt like trudging through jell-o, to the point that it seemed hopeless to try any longer. Suddenly, she awoke, kicking off her sheets and punching the air around her, battling something that could not be seen.

Christina got out of bed and walked to the kitchen for a glass of water. Her hand trembled uncontrollably, and water spilled on her nightshirt as she attempted to calm her nerves with a comedy show. Hours later, she finally fell asleep on the sofa, where she remained until the following morning.

A few nights later, she experienced a similarly unsettling dream, but this time, about Charlie. She had brought him to a pool for swim lessons and after dropping him off with the coach, walked over to a nearby picnic bench to watch. He trod water, swam from the pool wall to the instructor, and dove into the deep end, coming back up on his own shortly after. She remembered feeling proud of how well he could swim. Quite comfortable with how the lesson was going, she grabbed a romance novel from the swim bag and began to read. Minutes later, her concentration was broken by yells for an ambulance, and a crowd quickly gathered around someone lying on the ground. She frantically looked for Charlie but could no longer see him in the pool. It was only when she reached the onlookers that she realized, horrified, that he was the person on the ground. She could hear sirens in the distance growing closer. "Just breathe, baby," she begged, holding his hand as the coach performed CPR when suddenly, a large gulp of water was expelled from his lungs. He took a big gasp and, through his pale, blue lips, yelled, "They tried to get me!" Charlie was visibly shaking and cold to the touch as Christina pulled him up into her arms.

"Calm down, sweetie. You're okay now."

"Monster!" he yelled.

The instructor explained to the arriving paramedics that she and Charlie had been practicing when, suddenly and inexplicably, he was pulled towards the bottom of the deep end. It had taken two lifeguards to bring him back up.

Christina awoke with a start, breathing a sigh of relief when she found Charlie safe in his bed. She sat up for some time, thinking about her dreams and any possible meaning behind them. She wondered whether they were warnings of an imminent physical attack and possible poolside tragedy if she stayed in Manhattan. Perhaps they were a sign that she needed to consider moving to Statham Island. She would call Annette in the morning, she decided, and ask about touring the property.

Once again, she found herself sleeping on the sofa. It was closer to the kids' room, and she found it comforting to be near them, especially now.

Chapter Two

Two weeks later, Christina, Charlie, and Chelsea climbed aboard a small ferry called The Stargaze Express. The ferry normally traveled between touristy areas along East Hampton, but today, it had been rented by Annette for the purpose of taking the Martins to Statham Island, or Statham Manor, an interchangeable reference to the property she frequently toggled between. The idea of leaving everything behind to take over a large renovation project had grown on Christina, especially as the news of John and Rachel's engagement and pregnancy sunk in. Up until that point, she had half hoped that their marriage would survive, but knowing now that it never could, she desperately needed a task to keep her life moving forward. Her nightmares and growing fear that something bad would happen to her family if she stayed in Manhattan further fueled the desire to leave. Christina had talked with the twins about possibly moving to the island but wanted to visit first to ensure the move would work for them, too.

It was a Friday afternoon and the last day of school before the start of summer vacation. Christina had picked up the twins from their private school around noon in her black Volvo SUV, and they made the three-hour drive from Manhattan along I-495 East, across Long Island to East Hampton. As they drove along Main Street, they observed quaint little shops and nineteenth-century homes, surrounded by beautiful gardens and evergreens. The children grew excited when they passed Old Hook Mill, a two-century-year-old windmill, and its abutting graveyard. Growing up in Manhattan, they had rarely seen gravestones except when their street was decorated for Halloween. Chelsea asked where all of the pumpkins and skeletons were, obviously surprised that they were not amongst the gravestones, which made Christina chuckle.

Driving through town brought back memories of weekend getaways with John before the twins were born. They had enjoyed staying at bed and breakfasts and wandering the town over long weekends. Until this point, she had remembered those trips fondly but now felt a twinge of sadness returning to her old stomping grounds. She reminded herself that new memories could be made here, this time with the children.

Statham Island sat two miles offshore, and when Christina had discussed with John the possibility of moving with the children to the island, she described it generally as 'East Hampton' given its close proximity. John had seemed open to the idea of her taking the twins all summer, as his focus at the moment was on Rachel. The two were looking to buy a home and spent nearly every available weekend looking at properties. It was clear the twins' approval of the new home factored in little to the couple's decision.

Charlie had carried his backpack, containing library books and a school tablet that he had conveniently forgotten to return, aboard the ferry. He planned to have plenty of entertainment should the island visit turn out to be a bore. He also had candy and a cupcake left over from end-of-school-year celebrations, which he ate gloatingly in front of his sister, as he pulled out a book about turtles. His slick, dark hair and thin frame were nearly identical to John's. But despite the close resemblance, Charlie was an introverted little boy who struggled to make friendships. He found solace in his books and carried stories with him wherever he went.

Chelsea was very outgoing and had many friends in school. And while Charlie looked like John, she and her father shared the same personality. She preferred chatting to learning and been in trouble many times at school for not following directions. Her red, curly hair blew in the wind as she moved away from Charlie and closer to her mother at the front of the boat. She did not want to miss any part of the trip. She squealed with delight when the ferry blew its horn and began to move from the shore. The gorgeous beachfront summer homes of the wealthiest New Yorkers grew smaller and smaller until they resembled the tiny pieces of a Monopoly game.

"What's going to happen to Donna? We aren't going to just leave her there, are we?" Charlie asked his mom, referring to the name he and Chelsea had given the Volvo.

"She'll just wait for us until we're ready to leave," Christina answered matter-of-factly, smiling at his empathy.

Chelsea made her way back over to Charlie, and the two raced to point out other boats in the water. It was one of the first warm days of the season, although still quite chilly out on the water with the breeze. The two huddled together, happy they still had on their school uniform sweatshirts to block the wind.

"Do you think it's haunted?" Chelsea asked, thinking about the old manor they were about to explore.

"No, ghosts aren't real!" Charlie shot back, very serious in his expression. Although he still would not want to be in an old house alone, just in case.

"Well, I bet it has rats." Chelsea enjoyed seeing Charlie's reactions, and as predicted, he defensively claimed that the house had no rats, and if it did, they would only bite her.

Christina listened with amusement to the chatter as they moved closer to the island that was no longer so distant. The structures on the property that, from far away, had been indistinguishable from each other, now had their own defining traits, although lush greenery made it difficult to see the full extent of the land. A small forest of trees sat separated from the ocean by a rocky and sandy shoreline, and a cliff approximately twenty feet high stood on the far side of the property. It was becoming clear just how vast this property actually was. Annette had mentioned that it sat on twenty-two acres of land, but it looked much larger in person than she had imagined it would. Christina wondered why such a beautiful property with so much potential had such poor luck selling, especially in the Hamptons. Was Annette asking too much for it? Were there foundation issues? Did the area flood? Were there indeed rats? She promised herself that she would look for cracks in the foundation, be on alert for signs of mildew and mold, and pay extra attention to signs of infestations. She did not want to end up in a situation more overwhelming than her current one and decided that if the house did indeed have significant issues that would require an extraordinary amount of effort to remedy or threaten their health in some way, she was out of this role completely. She would turn around, hop back on the ferry, wish Annette well, and go home. That would be that.

A woman waved from the dock. From a distance, she almost looked to be walking on water due to the high tide. She wore a white shirt tucked neatly into high-waisted jeans and tan sandals. Her brown hair hung loosely, just past her shoulders. It was not often Christina saw her friend dressed so casually. She returned the wave. The ferry docked shortly after, causing the water around it to ripple and splash against the shoreline. The lapping of the waves continued as the three de-boarded, and Christina and Annette greeted each other with a quick embrace.

"How was your trip? I hope traffic wasn't too terrible and that the kids behaved," she said jokingly, giving Charlie a little nudge and causing him to giggle.

"Hi, Luke," she said, addressing the captain of the ferry. He was a young man in his mid-twenties and the son of the ferry owner. He smiled politely and waved.

"Well, I behaved, but Chelsea didn't," he said proudly. "She thinks that house is haunted and that rats live there. Well, they don't," he stated firmly, to which Annette laughed.

Chelsea gave Charlie's leg a little kick. "Do too," she said, almost inaudibly.

"Once we got out of the city, traffic was much better. The drive was beautiful, especially this time of year. But I could use some coffee after that long drive!" Annette had known Christina would want afternoon coffee and already had a pot brewing. After years of friendship and working together, she was all too familiar with Christina's coffee-drinking habits.

The group followed Annette off the pier and through a rusted, ivy-covered, iron arch that bore the name Statham Manor along the top. They traversed a small section of woods, overgrown with brush, and upon reaching the grassy clearing, were greeted by the sight of an expansive, stone manor reminiscent of an old English estate. A brick, circular drive occupied the front of the home with a large concrete fountain and flowers in need of weeding at its center. Wide-breadth stairs, surrounded by lion statues, paved the way to a set of large double doors, and the mystery of what lied behind those doors made Christina feel giddy, as though she were a child at Christmas time.

"Wow!" Christina exclaimed, unable to hide her excitement. She had wanted to see the estate for years and was taken aback by what she saw already. She counted seven windows spanning the second floor, and noted that the manor extended back quite a distance. A large portion of the manor sat covered in ivy that ran up the exterior walls, nearly reaching the roofline. Annette had been right about the roof needing to be repaired. The shingles were worn and missing, and she could see exposed wood around at least one of the attic's dormer windows, although surprisingly, none of the windows appeared to be broken. Despite the wear and tear, it was a marvelous structure that lived up to the manor title and could be absolutely breathtaking if restored properly.

"It's beautiful, isn't it? Statham Manor was built in 1880, which makes it older than the Statue of Liberty. Isn't that something?" she said, facing the twins. "But as you can probably see, it needs a little fixing up. I bet you two would be a big help to your mom if you decide to live here!" The twins nodded. They hardly noticed the overgrown landscape or peeling paint on the front doors. To them, it was a castle.

The group ascended the concrete stairs and waited patiently as Annette struggled to open the front doors, but after some finagling, they finally budged. Humidity had warped the wood, and Annette explained that the doors had a habit of getting stuck. Once the doors opened, it became clear that the interior had fared far better than the exterior. The high-ceiling foyer led to a grand staircase and spacious rooms on either side. Mid-century wallpaper adored the walls and was peeling off in several places, and the hardwoods were scuffed and needed refinishing, but those problems were easy enough to repair. Christina hoped that the rest of the house was in as good of shape and that the majority of the renovations would be purely aesthetic.

"Let me run and get the coffee!" Annette disappeared for a few minutes and reappeared with two cups, one for herself and the other for Christina. She handed juice boxes to the twins. Given the amount of touring to accomplish, the two women decided to carry their coffee around with them as they walked the house.

"Here, to the left, we have a formal living room." The room was furnished with two sitting areas and had a large marble fireplace with a framed oil painting of a man riding a horse above. "And over here, the library." The library sat behind the living room. It was a two-story, circular room with dark oak shelving, filled with books from floor to ceiling. A rail and movable ladder spanned the circumference of the room, making it possible to reach the higher shelves. The children's mouths dropped in awe at the sight of so many books, and they wondered if these were the boring books that only grownups read or if there were stories for kids, too. A couple of wooden desks and chairs sat in the middle of the room and reminded the twins of their school library. There was even a balcony, which stood on the second floor overlooking the group. "Do you like reading?"

Charlie answered enthusiastically, "Yeah!"

"Then you're going to love the little reading nook up there!" she said, pointing to the balcony. "We'll take a look at it when we go upstairs."

The group walked across the home, passing the grand staircase in the process. Its ornately carved banister and balusters were reminiscent of other Victorian-era homes that Christina had seen in the East Hampton area. Intricate and masterfully-carved depictions adorned the walls of the stairway and looked to depict a town. The fine detailing drew her in for a moment before Annette's voice brought her back to reality.

"Here is the dining room." The formal room sat across from the living room and contained an impressive oil painting gallery amongst its wainscoting. While some paintings were of the manor and its gardens, most were portraits, which Christina presumed to be of prior owners and their families. One painting in particular caught her attention. It was of a small boy, no older than Charlie, smiling and looking down at several kittens strewn about his lap and the grass on which he sat. A dish of milk sat beside him. She found the painting delightful and began to imagine the joy her own children might experience living at Statham Manor.

Christina noted another large marble fireplace, identical to the one in the living room, and pictured the occupants of the gallery sitting around the twelve-seat table for dinner with a cozy fire to keep warm. How many fancy dinner parties had been held in this room? And how long had it been since the home had last seen any signs of joy? Despite its undeniable beauty and luxury, there was a visible darkness about the home. The lamps glowed quite dimly, and the bright, sunny day did not seem to make its way indoors. Perhaps a simple window cleaning would brighten things up a bit, but deep down, Christina felt that something was amiss, though she could not quite put her finger on it. Perhaps the house was just in need of love, someone to care for and bring life back into it.

It became clear that the manor formed an L-shape, with the right side of the property extending far back. A long, unfurnished sunroom spanned the entire length of the house's side and contained a green tile fireplace and a grand wall of windows, making it one of the brightest rooms of the house. Across from the sunroom sat a cigar room, complete with brown leather chairs, ashtrays, and a dark oak fireplace. Annette explained that this would have been the room that the men gathered in after dinner to talk about politics and business, and Christina could almost smell the scent of cigar smoke and whiskey lingering in the air.

"Want to see a neat trick?" Annette asked the children. They jumped excitedly, eager to see what other mysteries the manor held. She carefully lifted a large painting off the wall and set it gently on the ground.

"Whoa!" exclaimed Charlie. "What is that?"

"It's a safe. It's where wealthy owners of this manor used to hide their valuables so that no one would take them," she explained.

"What are values?" asked Chelsea.

"Valuables are things that are important to you. For the people who used to live here, it was probably money and jewelry." The kids began to imagine the fancy owners who lived in the home. They pictured them as royalty wearing fur coats and crowns and a safe full of jewels and gold coins.

"How were they wealthy?" Christina asked, intrigued by the couple who built the home.

"I believe they were in oil. That's all Uncle Bob told me, anyway."

Walking back towards the grand staircase to see the upper floors, Christina realized that she had not seen any air vents in the manor. Annette explained that her uncle had planned to install a ventilation system but passed away before he could do so. "But the home does stay very warm in winter with the use of the fireplaces, as you can imagine, and the breezes from the water cool the home nicely in summer."

Christina wondered where the kitchen was. She had not seen it on the first floor. Annette explained that the main kitchen was in the basement, while a smaller one would be part of their suite in the attic. "A long time ago, hired staff would cook for the family living in the home, and kitchens at that time were often in basements to be out of the way and closer to the root cellar, where food was typically stored in large quantities."

"What if you wanted a snack at night?" Charlie asked.

"Well, you'd have to walk all the way to the basement," Christina mused.

The second floor contained seven fully-furnished suites, each with a fireplace, bedroom, bathroom, and sitting area. Christina found no traces of rodent droppings or mold, and besides old wallpaper, outdated bathrooms, and worn hardwoods, there was nothing notable about the space. She wondered how many guests had stayed in these rooms throughout the years.

Christina opened the last wooden door on the floor and was surprised to find the library balcony, which she had nearly forgotten about. It was small but cozy, just as Annette had promised. It contained a single wooden desk matching the desks below and was flanked on either side by smaller bookcases that would indeed be more accessible should they choose to use the space. Christina had not noticed it until now, but a line of windows ran along the top of the library, supplying a great deal of natural light. What a wonderful place to read, she thought. She understood perfectly why the builders had created such a space. Winters in the Northeast were notoriously dark and cold. But no matter the weather, this indoor library balcony could, in essence, give the feeling of being outdoors and, like the sunroom, must have acted as an antidote to winter blues during colder months.

The old wooden staircase extended to the attic, where a furnished suite spanned the entire right side of the house. It would be the living quarters for the family while renovations were being completed and had two bedrooms, a bathroom, a sitting area with a fireplace, and a small kitchen of its own. The furnishings were more extravagant than those in the rest of the manor. Annette explained that in years past, the attic had been the preferred living space of the owners, given its panoramic views that spanned nearly the entire property. Looking East were gardens; North was the town of East Hampton, off in the distance; West was a large greenhouse; and South were secluded beaches. The way in which the light shone through the windows cast the image of waves on the ceiling and made Christina feel as though she was on a boat. And as she stood watching the waves dance above her, she noticed it. Dark splotches, surrounded by water stains, ran along the kitchen ceiling from the fridge to the sink. There was a roof leak and an active one at that. The ceiling was soft and still wet to the touch. It was clear that this was an area lying underneath damaged roofing, and tearing out and replacing the drywall was added to the mental tally of work to do. Annette assured her that the room would be blocked off from the children until the mold had been removed and that fixing the mold issue would take priority over other projects. Christina closed the kitchen door behind them, and they all took some time to enjoy the views. Annette had cracked open one of the dormer windows, and a welcome, soft breeze rolled through, cooling the warm room and drying the sweat that was beaded on their foreheads.

Charlie had been growing fidgety and slipped away, undetected from the group, to explore the attic himself. The tour no longer interested him, as the adults spent most of it discussing renovations. He wondered what was behind some of the closed doors of the attic; perhaps the family had left behind toys or even treasures. He wandered into the hallway and through a door on the other side of the staircase. The room was dark, its only illumination coming from the dwindling afternoon sunlight that streamed through the windows in slight, dim beams. He could not locate a light switch but could see just well enough to find his way around. The room smelled of aged wood and reminded him of an old barn he had recently visited while on a class field trip. As his eyes adjusted, he noticed exposed wood beams running along the roof line…and then, something else. The dimming sunlight seemed to catch the outline of a large object a few feet away. He stared for a moment, unsure of what his eyes had spotted, and gulped when he saw the fur and large claws. A bear, he thought, but his rational mind told him he was mistaken since bears lived in the woods and in caves, not in old manors. But around the animal were several sets of eyes belonging to smaller, but equally terrifying, bodies. They stood together, still and silent, watching his every move, like a pack of wolves ready to attack. His heart began to race as he slowly backed away, and as he neared the door, there was a shuffle that was not his own, followed by movement amongst the lifeless animals. But it was not the animals that moved. It was something else. The animals stared at Charlie, terror in their eyes, yet paralyzed in fear. Then it moved again. A tall, shadowy figure, slithered between the creatures and across the room, and then, much to Charlie's terror, walked through the wall and disappeared on the far side of the room.

A shriek pierced the air, and suddenly realizing that Charlie was missing, Christina jumped. Where had he gone? Chelsea had fallen asleep on the sofa while the women chatted, and Christina had just assumed that he had been playing or reading close by.

"He can't have gone far," Annette said, getting up to help look.

"Charlie, where are you?" She tried to remain calm but suddenly began to panic, fearing that he might have gone back to the library balcony and perhaps fallen off the railing onto the floor below. "Charlie!" She ran down the stairs to the balcony but could not see him anywhere. Another terrified scream, the type a parent knows to be one of sheer terror or pain. Christina realized it was coming from right above her, and she raced back up the stairs to find Annette running across the hallway and into a room that she had not yet seen. A light flipped on, and there sat Charlie, curled into a ball, shaking and crying. It quickly became clear why he was so terrified. A taxidermy collection, consisting of a large bear, foxes, deer, and birds, filled the room, and having never seen preserved animals before, Charlie probably thought he had wandered into a jungle. Christina hugged him and held him tight. Annette felt terrible that she had not thought to warn Christina of that room before they went upstairs but had not expected Charlie to roam around on his own.

"I want to go home," he finally mustered in a weak voice. He was still trembling.

"They're not real, sweetheart. See." She touched the bear, playfully jumping backward as if suddenly scared, and then poked him, hoping to get a laugh. But Charlie did not so much as crack a smile. Christina explained that the animals were preserved and could not hurt him, so there was nothing to be scared of. But her words did little to comfort him.

Charlie insisted that one of the animals was alive. He had seen it move. Knowing that his imagination must have gotten the best of him, Christina reassured him that the animals could not move and had been in the same spot for decades. But he knew what he had seen. Something *had* moved. He did not like that room, not one bit. There was something unsavory and threatening about it. As he exited, his mom's arm around his shoulder, he promised himself that he would never go back into that room again. Annette looked uncomfortably around and then closed the door behind them, giving it a jostle to ensure it was tightly latched.

Chelsea met them in the hallway, having awoken from the commotion. "Is Charlie okay?"

"He's fine, darling," Christina assured, but Chelsea could see that he had been crying. She followed as the group entered the adjacent observatory, peeking at Charlie every so often, but he avoided looking back in her direction. The room was empty, except for an old-fashioned telescope held by a wooden tripod that stood aimed towards the dormer windows.

"In the late 1800s, this telescope was one of the most sophisticated pieces of equipment at the time. And the lack of city lights made this an ideal spot for observing the planets," Annette relayed. And then, turning to the twins, she motioned for them to follow. "Now, I have a surprise for you! Check this out!"

A door, which one might expect to be a hall closet, sat inconspicuously at the end of the hallway. Annette opened it, yanking a pull-string light to an old, flickering wall-mounted bulb, revealing a hidden wooden stairwell, its unfinished treads worn from years of use. Looking down, they could see that it wound around and around all the way to the basement. "These steps were once used by staff of the family who owned the manor as a way to keep their presence minimized," she explained. Chelsea repeated the word 'minized,' not understanding what it meant. The kids were shocked to learn that the home had seven staircases in all…two between each floor, as well as one from the basement to the outside.

The stairwell had a similar exit on each floor before terminating in the basement, revealing a large space with stone walls and floors and divided into rooms. A large kitchen took up nearly half of the area. Its dated appliances, which included an old wood-burning oven, had Christina wondering how she was going to cook without setting the house on fire. Annette reassured her that all of the appliances were in working order, although she planned to replace them during renovations. A small laundry room sat just off the kitchen with a washer and dryer that looked usable enough. And towards the back of the basement sat a row of four staff quarters, which presumably were used by the maids and butlers in years past. Each room had no more than a simple cot and dresser with an old kerosene lamp atop and had obviously sat neglected for decades.

The twins asked to play outside before it got too dark and were left on the brick drive to enjoy the last of the day's warm sunlight. Christina gave them explicit instructions to stay there while she and Annette walked the property. She did not want them to wander off and get lost, or worse, make it to the water front. Both nodded their heads as they received instructions, and Christina figured they would be safe for a short time as they explored the grounds.

"When my uncle bought the property, it was in horrible shape. No one had kept it up in years. But he was able to do quite a bit of projects before he passed away." She was proud of the dent her uncle had made in the immense renovating project. "But as you can see, there's still so much to do. I was hoping someone would want a project and be willing to purchase as is, but apparently, you and I are the only ones who don't mind fixing homes up these days," she laughed. The two walked towards a path along the tree line, passing a greenhouse that sat to the right of the manor. A significant number of glass panels had broken when a tree fell onto it some years earlier. Although the tree had long since been removed, the greenhouse had never been repaired or even cleaned up, and broken glass sat scattered around the structure.

"This path goes around the entire island and is about one-mile long. It's great for bike rides and walks!" The path remained clear of plant growth, having been salted in the past, and was surprisingly easy to navigate considering the mess that plagued other areas of the property.

They followed the trail, ending up on the backside of the manor. "Is that another pier?" Christina asked, pointing towards a wooden walkway along the shoreline.

"It is! And the private beach area is one of the prettiest on the island. There is less boating activity on this side, so it's far quieter than where you came in. There are some edible berry bushes that grow along the edge of the beach, and the last time I was over there, the sand had quite a few seashells that I'm sure Charlie and Chelsea would enjoy hunting for."

The two passed a ridge of established cypress trees and then came upon a large garden filled with bushes, flowers, stone paths, and a fountain. Christina imagined how beautiful it must have looked when maintained. She could see the back of the L-shaped manor and realized that the large grassy field behind the house was enclosed by rose bushes, creating a natural courtyard. And for the first time, she noticed another stone structure sitting hidden at the far end of the property. It had a large steeple spanning high above the roofline and reminded her of a church.

"Does this place really have its own chapel?" Christina asked, excited that she might have access to a private place of worship if she lived on the island. Annette confirmed that it was, indeed, a church and promised to show it to her when they returned, but Christina detected a certain hesitance in her voice. Perhaps Annette had plans later and simply wanted to finish up the tour, she thought to herself.

The path weaved through the garden back towards the house and then back again towards the shore, leading them past a second, smaller garden with large stone slab walkways and rose-covered archways of its own. And winding back again, they passed an irregular-shaped pool, its water muddied and lily pads peaking above the surface. One could easily mistake it for a natural pond at this point. The concrete patio around the pool was devoid of the lounge chairs one would typically expect in a pool area, and the grass had encroached over much of the concrete, almost as if nature was attempting to claim the area as its own. Annette assured Christina that she would not be expected to drain or refill the water as a separate company had already been hired to clean it.

The final quarter mile provided picturesque views of the Atlantic Ocean and the distant shoreline of Long Island. The ferry patiently waited to their right. The captain was eating a sandwich, his feet propped up comfortably, and he waved as they walked past and then back towards the manor. The tour had been longer than

Christina anticipated, and she was relieved to find the twins still playing where she left them. They had picked up sticks and were having a "sword" fight, laughter filling the air as they swung at each other. Charlie seemed to have completely forgotten about the events in the attic that afternoon.

"Mind if we look at the church?" she reminded Annette.

She had hoped that Christina had forgotten about the building. "Sure. This way," Annette said, hiding her reluctance behind a polite smile.

She and the Martins walked the short distance to the area behind the home. Despite being overgrown with weeds and vines, Christina could see the potential of the space and felt eager to clean it up. The rose bushes surrounding the yard gave it a sweet scent, and off in the corner sat the small stone chapel. Annette explained that the original inhabitants had been devout Catholics and attended services daily. She believed they had actually even hired a priest to live on the land. But over the years, the building had fallen into disrepair. She opened a set of double doors, behind which sat several pews with an altar at the helm and a large crucifix behind it. Two oil paintings, one of Mary holding baby Jesus and the other of Jesus and his disciples at the Last Supper, hung on either side. The water-damaged ceiling had once been masterfully painted in religious imagery, reminiscent of the Sistine Chapel, beautifully offset from the now-peeling, white-painted stone walls. Despite the damage, it was easy to see the potential of the chapel and the grandeur it once held. But any desire to look around further was quickly thwarted by a repulsive odor of mustiness and rot that sent the group back out as soon as they entered. Annette quickly slammed the chapel doors shut behind them and hunched over, as if she was going to be sick.

"Oh my God. That's awful," Christina said aloud, trying desperately to control her own nausea. "Something must have died in there."

"I'm sorry. As you can see, there is one area of the island that is not so desirable."

"It's horrible," Christina corrected. She had never been inside a church that had felt so oppressive…evil even, and she felt relieved when Annette told her it would be torn down. Until then, she forbade the children to go back without her.

The setting sun cast rays of yellow and orange on the ground, as if creating a path for their walk back to the manor. Once they reached the front steps, Annette gestured towards the home. "So what do you think? Do you want to take it on?"

Christina had decided before visiting the island that if renovations were manageable enough, she would. And John's apathy towards raising the kids solidified her choice. "I'll do it," she said, smiling, feeling excited about something for the first time in months. She hoped that this would be a positive start to post-married life and provide a much-needed break from the hectic career that had consumed her. But she also hoped to be able to show Charlie and Chelsea perseverance in the face of adversity and to give them their own break from reality, even if just for a summer.

"Great, I'm glad to have you here! And you guys, too," she said to the twins with a grin. Despite Annette's desperate desire to sell and sever her ties with the property, she was genuinely happy to help her friend in the process.

They talked briefly about what needed to be done to fix up the manor and its grounds. There was the mold removal, roofing repair, wallpaper replacement, painting, gardening, bathroom and kitchen remodels, floor refinishing, greenhouse repair, and church teardown. Annette asked that all projects be run by her before they were started, while Christina would manage the contractors in their day-to-day operations, acting as Annette's stand-in. Christina was very driven and had always been able to solve problems, no matter what came her way, and felt confident that she would be able to oversee the undertaking without too many hiccups.

"Forgive me for asking, but how will the contractors transport heavy materials to the island?" Christina asked. She imagined that a passenger ferry would be unwilling to move the large amount of waste created in a renovation as well.

"Every construction group that I've spoken with has a barge on hand. There are many islands like Statham in these waters, although most are on smaller plots with tiny cabins, so I'm guessing they are used to it."

It was decided that work would begin the week after next and run until some point in the Fall. The kids would have to live with John for a few weeks once school began, and that was a subject she would bridge with him on Tuesday when they planned to meet to discuss the division of parental roles.

It was dinnertime, and they needed to head back to the mainland if they were to make it back to Manhattan that night. Christina felt bad that Luke had been waiting aboard the ferry for several hours, but Annette assured her that she was paying him handsomely for his time.

"You are more than welcome to stay the night," Annette offered, but the twins had a birthday party to attend the following morning.

The four walked back to the ferry and hopped aboard. Annette had plans to stay at a bed and breakfast off Main Street that night, which Christina thought odd given her access to such a beautiful manor, but figured that she had her reasons. Perhaps she had a date or just wanted the adventure of exploring a new hotel.

Annette was the type of person to always be doing something different.

Statham Island became smaller in the distance, and fifteen minutes later, they were back along the shore of East Hampton. Donna had waited for them, just as Christina had promised Charlie, and soon, they were past the quaint town of East Hampton and on their way home.

Annette had been excited to show off the property but hoped that it was the last time she would have to give a tour. The property had become an unwanted burden and she was eager to renew her focus on work and spend her weekends within the city. She had lost her farm roots of her youth long ago and these days, would rather attend shows and enjoy restaurants than be surrounded by the offsetting quietness of nature. It made her feel uneasy to not have people around at all times, and even more unsettled when she did not feel that uneasiness on Statham Island.

Chapter Three

John and Christina met at a Starbucks the following Tuesday to divide out Charlie and Chelsea's care for the next few months. John ordered a Matcha Lemonade as he was not particularly fond of coffee. He had only agreed to meet at the coffee house because it was an easy, neutral location, and he could quickly leave should conversations grow sour. Christina ordered a Grande Caffe Americano, black. A warm June breeze blew her freshly highlighted hair off her shoulders, and John had to catch himself as he admired her beauty. Their divorce, now finalized, had formally stipulated that the children remain with Christina during the week and visit John on weekends. But the former couple had mutually decided, at least for the moment, to reconvene every few weeks to work around John's flying schedule and Christina's move to the island. John was happy to send the children off for the summer as life with Rachel took up most of his free time. Christina had accepted her role as a single mother and, given her lowered expectations for his involvement, was pleasantly surprised when he talked about the house he had just purchased with Rachel and its extra rooms for the twins when they visited. She had half expected them to sleep on the sofa.

Earlier that morning, Christina had submitted paperwork to the courthouse requesting that her last name be changed back to her maiden name, Taylor. She no longer wanted to be known as Mrs. Martin. The sharpness of the pain caused by John had ruined the name that she once used proudly. When she said goodbye to John in the coffee shop, she no longer felt the need to fight with or for him. Working out childcare had become equivalent to acting as a legal mediator between doctors and patients. There was no room for emotion; only problem solving and moving on to the next task.

She found it difficult to imagine what had kept them married for so long. With the marriage behind her, she could finally see their life together with clarity, and the rot that permeated the very foundation of their relationship was ever so apparent. Like a rug over a water-damaged floor, she had worked hard to cover up the damage, and for so long, her marriage had appeared to be the storybook picture of happiness. But in reality, it had been a façade, behind which was a pain that had aged her and taken a piece of her soul.

Finally, she felt free to enjoy life again, and resuming the title of Ms. Taylor was at the heart of her transition.

The night before the move, she felt a sense of nostalgia as she packed up the last of the belongings from the apartment. She and John had mutually decided to sell the apartment, John in order to help with the down payment on his new house, and Christina because she simply could not bear to live there anymore. She and John had made the purchase when they first got married, and it had been their home for the past nine years. But despite the pleasant memories, it was also a reminder of John. The paint colors he chose and the light fixtures he installed made the apartment feel like it would always be his.

Christina had taken the step of selling her portion of the firm that she had helped to establish. Years and years of tireless work had gone into creating a top-notch medical malpractice group, and suddenly, she did not want it. She knew she could never be happy continuing to do what she had done for so long, and once she was certain that Statham Island was going to work out for the kids, she met with her fellow partner and broke the news. He had assumed that it was the divorce driving this decision, but in reality, Christina had experienced a great awakening and, for the first time, had been able to take a step back and decide whether she wanted to continue practicing at the top of her field or make some risky changes that ultimately would bring her more life fulfillment.

The next morning, Pete wished them well, giving all three hugs, as they walked out of the apartment entrance for the last time. A tear rolled down his cheek as he helped load the last of their luggage into the car and gave Charlie and Chelsea high fives. He would miss them all, but especially the children. "Goodbye, Pete," called Chelsea, just as she did every morning before school. She gave him one of her sweet smiles and waved as they drove off in Donna. Charlie was more somber and quiet during the ride. He wondered whether they were going to see him again or if it was going to be like when their grandfather died, and they had to wait until they got to Heaven.

The little ferry sat waiting at the dock when they arrived several hours later. The weather had forecasted rain that afternoon, and Christina was relieved to see the sun shining when they arrived in East Hampton. The three boarded, this time carrying suitcases filled with clothes, toiletries, stuffed animals, and the books that Charlie had specifically asked to bring. Charlie had given back the school tablet before leaving and pulled out a book about dinosaurs to read during the short trip. Chelsea held a small camera that she received for her last birthday, hoping to catch a photo of a shark to show her father. And Christina carried several bags of groceries, medicine, bandages, topical ointments, and cleaning supplies, not knowing exactly what would already be at the house once they arrived. Annette had given her the keys the day before and had no intention of returning to the property until remodeling was completed.

The property appeared just as majestic as the first time they saw it. But the weather had warmed and overgrowth multiplied in just a few weeks' time. Beyond the dock and sandy shoreline sat thick, lush greenery that encroached upon the walkway leading up to the house, which now sat behind fully-bloomed forestry. As they walked up the brick drive, she could see that the ivy growing along the home had grown to fully cover two top windows.

Christina remembered that the front door took some finagling on their last visit, and today was no different. The key turned easily, but indeed, the warped door took some forceful shoving to budge, creaking as it swung open. Inside, the house appeared just as they had seen it before, and with the long day of traveling behind them, they all eagerly walked in.

"Well, guys, welcome to our new home!" Christina exclaimed, excited as they started a new chapter in their lives. It was a beautiful manor on an enchanting island with so much promise. "Isn't it beautiful? How did we get so lucky?" She squeezed the twins closer as she took in a deep breath and admired the stately structure around her.

"Can we eat now?" whined Chelsea, somewhat less interested in the manor than on their first visit. "I'm hungry." It had been a long drive, and she had missed breakfast that morning.

Charlie was eager to investigate the manor once again, and lunch was at the bottom of his list of concerns. But Christina agreed that they needed to unload groceries and eat before they did anything else.

"Chelsea, Charlie, carry these downstairs," she said, handing each a grocery bag. "You remember where the kitchen is? I'll be down in a moment." She wanted to do a quick walk around the house to make sure there were no broken windows, dead vermin, or anything else unexpected before the kids started to run around and play. As she walked room to room, she opened the windows that were not jammed, letting in a sweet, cool breeze to offset the stuffiness and warmth inside.

A pleasant surprise awaited her in the basement. The refrigerator and large separate freezer already sat fully stocked with fresh food. There was a vast array of fresh fruits, vegetables, dairy products, eggs, and breads in the refrigerator, as well as frozen meats and precooked TV dinners in the freezer. The root cellar stood stocked with canned and jarred items, enough to last at least several months, and a large pantry was filled with paper towels, toilet paper rolls, and dry goods, including cereals, snacks, and baking ingredients, in addition to the groceries the twins had dutifully unloaded.

A letter from Annette sat on the counter:

Dear Christina,

Thank you for stepping forward to help with this large endeavor. I hope that the island treats you and the children well.

As you may have realized by now, the kitchen is fully stocked. I literally purchased the entire inventory from Sam's Grocery, so you are welcome!

The ferry will deliver additional groceries and household supplies once a week on Thursdays at 2:00 as a standing time. Mike is the ferry owner and easy to get a hold of. Call him if you need additional deliveries or want to leave the island, but it is expensive, so keep that in mind.

J&J Contracting will be out Monday morning to start renovations. Also, I padlocked the taxidermy room, so you won't have to worry about Charlie or Chelsea wandering in. We will talk soon.

XOXO,

Annette

Christina made a quick meal of canned corn, instant potatoes, and frozen chicken nuggets served with apple juice for the twins and herself. She had become accustomed to eating the same food as the kids and had not cooked an adult meal since John moved out. She was relieved to find that all of the kitchen appliances worked, just as Annette had promised. They would have to last until the mold in the attic kitchen had been mitigated.

Charlie and Chelsea were eager to explore their new home and ran off right after eating, leaving Christina to clean up and unpack. She wasted no time hauling luggage up to the attic, and once clothes were hung and folded away, she switched to cleaning surfaces and bathrooms. There was no telling when the manor had last been cleaned properly, and the thick layers of dust suggested it may have been years. Charlie and Chelsea played outside the front door, and she could hear their voices off in the distance as she worked. After nearly two hours, she was exhausted and decided to hold off on the mopping until the following day. It was starting to become dusk anyway, and she did not want the children playing outside past dark. They had only just arrived and were still learning their way around the grounds. And who knew whether there were any animals or, God-forbid, people living on the property?

That night, all three snuggled together in the main bedroom of the attic suite. Tomorrow, she would push the twins to sleep in the spare room, but just tonight, she would baby them. The twins did not even ask to watch their favorite cartoons or to be read a bedtime story and fell quickly asleep at her side. It reminded her of when they were toddlers and slept with her, curled into two tiny balls, whenever John was away on trips.

In the middle of the night, Christina and Charlie awoke to the screams and thrashes of Chelsea. The youngster had recently begun experiencing terrifying nightmares on an almost nightly basis, and the sleep interruptions were becoming trying for Christina, who held her tightly in her arms, rocking her gently back and forth in a routine she was now accustomed to performing. The terror in the child's face was difficult to watch. "Wake up, sweetie. Wake up. It's okay."

When she finally awoke, she sobbed uncontrollably, panting and shaking. It was only after several minutes that she was able to talk. "There were scary people in a church singing strange songs," she sobbed. "It looked like our church, but it wasn't. There was a creepy man with red eyes!" As she talked, more tears welled up in her eyes and rolled down her cheeks.

Christina decided not to push for information and just hugged her tighter as she talked.

"I know it seems scary, sweetie, but it was just a bad dream. And bad dreams happen to lots of people. Even Mama has bad dreams sometimes. But it's okay. There is nothing that is going to hurt you."

"But it's not just a dream. The man with the red eyes is real. He comes at night, and he's mean. He's going to hurt us." Her wide eyes conveyed that she truly believed the nightmares were real and that they were in danger, and Christina began to wonder if she should have addressed the nightmares with her pediatrician before they moved to the island. But there had simply been no time as she juggled the divorce, selling her portion of the firm, and packing. She had hoped the change of scenery and fresh start would bring an end to the phenomenon, and perhaps it still would. After all, they had just arrived that day.

"You know what I think? I think you two could use a cookie!" That was a trick she used to quickly calm their nerves after a nightmare episode. Predictably, a smile broke out on the twins' faces, and she rushed to the basement and grabbed a few cookies and milk. But when she returned a few minutes later, both had already fallen back asleep, huddled together in the middle of the bed. Christina gathered a blanket and pillow and snuggled into a chair, where she fell in and out of sleep for the remainder of the night.

The next morning, Christina awoke early. The open windows brought in the first of the sunlight, and she wanted to get a few things done before Chelsea and Charlie required her attention. She moved throughout the downstairs, mopping years of dirt and grime off the wood. The floors had evidently not been cleaned properly for some time, and the mop water was a dark grey by the time she finished the third floor. The kids were still sleeping when loud knocks came from the front of the house. There was no doorbell, so any visitors had to knock loudly to make their presence known. She wondered who would be stopping by as the construction crew was not due to start until the following Monday, and there were no neighbors to speak of. Furthermore, it was not the type of place that was easily reached. A sudden sense of fear took over as she wondered who it was and what they wanted, and fearing the worst, she grabbed a poker from a fireplace end route to the door.

"Who is it?" she called.

"It's Mike. From The Stargaze Express…the ferry company. I'm a friend of Annette's. You met my son, Luke, when you came out a few weeks ago."

Christina opened the door slowly, poker still in hand. Living in the city had made her ultra vigilant to crime risk, and being alone with two children only heightened her guard. An aging gentleman in his late sixties with balding hair and a gentle face stood on the other side of the door and did not appear to be any more threatening than a boy scout. In fact, something about him reminded her of Pete. He lowered his hat in greeting, and Christina put down the poker in embarrassment, extending her hand.

"It's nice to meet you. Annette asked me to stop by and check on you all…see how you're settling in."

"You'll have to excuse this," she said, pointing to the poker. "I guess I just haven't quite gotten used to living here yet, and I wasn't expecting anyone until next week. But it's nice to meet you too, Mike! Come in. Would you like tea or coffee?"

Just then, Chelsea and Charlie descended the large oak stairs towards the foyer, still dressed in their pajamas, Charlie carrying his favorite teddy bear.

"No, but thank you. I've had my fair share of coffee already," he said graciously. "Now, who are these little ones?"

"I'm Chelsea, and this is Charlie, my little brother."

"I'm not your *little* brother. We're twins," Charlie corrected, with a look of disdain at the mere thought of being younger than his sibling.

"Well, Mama says I was born first."

Mike pulled something out of his pocket. "Do you like lollipops?" he asked, pulling out two rainbow-colored pops that he bought that morning at the local coffee shop. "It is okay, isn't it?" he said, looking up at Christina.

"Of course." Christina gave him a thankful nod. "How about a little breakfast and *then* candy," she told the twins, who excitedly thanked Mike and ran downstairs to pour themselves cereal. "It was nice of you to stop by. I hope to be seeing you again soon."

"I'm here if you need anything. I will plan to come by on Thursday afternoons with groceries, but if there's an emergency, you can reach me at this number," he said, scribbling his contact information on a piece of scrap paper. "I can be back out here in a jiffy. Well, I'd better get back, but it was a pleasure to meet you."

"It was nice to meet you too, Mike." She closed the door, and once again, the house returned to silence except for the sounds of the children busily chomping on their breakfast.

Christina and the kids sat in the basement, looking around at the old kitchen. Its dated appliances reminded her of her grandmother's house; most were a lime-green color, except for the refrigerator, which was white and obviously much newer. Coffee was brewing, and she was looking forward to sitting with her cup in the library as she explored the old book collection.

The relative quietness was again broken by the sound of loud knocking on the front door. Had Mike forgotten something? Then another frantic knock, this time louder and more insistent. She told the children not to move and sprinted upstairs to the foyer. When she cracked open the door, she was shocked to find Mike in a terrible state, his plaid shirt ripped along the left arm and his khaki pants covered in dirt. She noticed that his right shoe was missing.

"What happened? Oh, my goodness! Come inside." She pulled him into the home and quickly shut the door behind him, locking the deadbolt as she did. Was someone or something chasing him, or was he having a medical emergency, she wondered. It suddenly occurred to her that there was no way paramedics could reach the island quickly. And if she transported Mike with the ferry, she would have to rely on him for driving instructions since she had no idea how to operate it. She helped him limp to one of the living room sofas, followed by Charlie and Chelsea, who had made their way upstairs, curious as to what all the commotion was. He was breathing deeply and sweating, and it took him a moment to speak.

"I'm sorry to bother you again," he apologized. "I was walking back to the ferry when I found myself surrounded by bees. Not just a couple. Tens of thousands of them, all along the property just before the woods. The swarm was so thick that I could hardly see the ground. They just seemed to come out of nowhere. I will never forget the sound of them all buzzing. I didn't have time to even move before I got attacked." Mike rolled up his sleeves, and Christina could see that they had stung up and down his arms. Several dead bees fell out his pant legs and onto the floor.

"I fell running back and twisted my ankle. And, you know, the strange thing is they were not there when I got here maybe half an hour ago."

Christina had not noticed any bees when they arrived the day prior. She had planned to let the children out to play while she cleaned and was relieved she had not.

Christina stood up. "You two, sit with Mike for a minute," she said, turning to the twins. Both were busily eating the lollipops Mike had given them earlier and did as their mother requested. "I'll be right back." She ran downstairs and returned shortly after with a cold soda, an ice pack, and Benadryl, handing them to Mike. It was then that she could see that his arms and face had started to swell. "Charlie, Chelsea, I need you to clean up your dishes from breakfast," she said, not wanting them to see how badly Mike was hurt. "Take this," she instructed, handing him the Benadryl. "It will make you feel much better." She was glad she had thought to pack a first aid kit as the house had not had one.

Half an hour passed, and the welts on Mike's body began to flatten. He and Christina cautiously approached the area by the wood line where the bees had been. Sure enough, tens of thousands of bees swarmed, just as Mike had described. Their movement made the land below look as if it was moving, and she found herself grabbing onto Mike's welted arm for balance.

"Oh my God!" she exclaimed. It was one thing to be told of the swarm but quite another to actually see it firsthand. "I will call someone. I'm so sorry about all of this."

"It's not your fault. I've never seen anything like this myself. Don't worry about calling around. It's Saturday, and you'll never get anyone out this weekend. My neighbor is a retired beekeeper, and I will ask him if he can come out today."

"Oh, I would appreciate that. Thank you."

"No problem."

"Are you okay to ferry back on your own?"

"I'm feeling much better. I think I'll just have to find a new path to the ferry, though." The two walked in a large semi-circle around the bees and towards the ferry, and Christina watched the boat until it was out of sight.

Later that evening, Mike's beekeeper friend arrived, as promised, dressed in protective clothing. He introduced himself as Jeff and told Christina that he had already distributed an insecticide.

"You'll want to avoid the general area for the next few days, at least until the next good rain. The bees should be gone pretty quickly," he conveyed.

"How much do I owe you?" Christina asked, thankful that he cared enough to arrive that very day.

"Nothing. In this town, we take care of each other. Just consider it a welcome gift," he replied, much to her surprise.

The next morning, most of the bees were dead, just as the beekeeper had promised. On the ground lied piles of dead insects and flocks of birds gathering to feast off their remains. She hoped that the poison would not hurt them as well, but the birds returned day after day, seemingly unaffected. Soon, she would almost forget that the bees had even been there at all.

Monday morning, it rained. It was the type of rain that comes in sideways and gets into every which corner, creating a damp chill that permeated the house. Christina and the twins found themselves looking through their clothes for pants and sweaters. In spite of the weather, three men from J&J Contracting showed up at nine o'clock sharp, ready to begin renovations on the property.

Jason and Jeremy were brothers and had founded the company nearly two decades prior while they were in their early twenties. They were two years apart and looked similar, both with short blonde hair and husky builds, and were often mistaken for each other. Originally from Alaska, they had grown up around shipping boats and had a love for the water. They found themselves in New York in short succession of each other. Jason was first and moved away from home to attend college at NYU. His love for the state of New York, as well as the niche getaway area of the Hamptons, lulled him into staying after graduation.

Jeremy found himself following in his brother's footsteps after their father suddenly died following a brief fight with pancreatic cancer. Their mother had passed away when they were young, and with the loss of their father, there was nothing left for him in Alaska. He had attended a community college but dropped out when Jason put forth the idea of starting the construction business.

The brothers had built up their company over the years and developed a strong reputation for their work, having renovated nearly thirty percent of the homes in the area. In fact, they were quite familiar with Statham Manor already and had actually been hired by Annette's uncle to fix a few odds and ends on the property. The men had developed a good relationship with Bob and were saddened to learn of his passing. It felt strange to return, given how much had transpired since they last worked there. The furniture and decorations were just as they remembered. It was only the overgrown landscape and deteriorating exterior that gave any indication that significant time had passed since their last visit. And the fact that one man in their crew was no longer with them. Albert had made his work on Statham Island his last with the company before suddenly and mysteriously leaving after fifteen years. No one had spoken to him since the day he announced his departure. That moment remained etched in the memories of Jason and Jeremy and filed away as one of the most bizarre incidents they had ever experienced. The barge had just docked following a long day at the manor when Albert announced, out of the blue, that he was leaving J&J Contracting and would not be returning. No explanation, not even a forwarding address for his last paycheck. Jason and Jeremy only discovered that he had moved when their letter with the check enclosed was returned to them by the postal service. His phone was disconnected, and he had no known family that they could contact. It was as though he had just vanished into thin air. The circumstances of Albert's disappearance continued to mystify the brother's years later.

Not long after his departure, they were fortunate enough to meet Sam. He was about the age that their father would have been with graying hair and a thinning frame and had been a great hire, despite his age. He was a hard worker and master carpenter, which proved an invaluable skill working within the older homes of East Hampton. He never complained and always arrived on time. Whenever Jeremy or Jason took time off, he was able to manage their roles and his own simultaneously, including when Jeremy's child was sick and back and forth to the doctor for several weeks, and then again when Jason suddenly found himself hospitalized with appendicitis. Sam had become a vital part of their team.

After brief introductions, Christina and the crew sat around the dining room table and discussed renovations and their respective priority levels. She was surprised to learn that Annette had already informed the contractors, in great detail, of what was to be done and that they were ready to start on the penthouse kitchen that very day.

The barge was loaded up with tools and materials covered by a large blue tarp, secured at the corners to the floor to keep the rain off during travel. She laid down towels in the foyer for the men's wet shoes to keep mud from being tracked all over her newly cleaned floors. By mid-afternoon, the house was alive with the sound of banging and hammering, and renovations at Statham Manor were officially underway.

Chapter Four

Each morning, the contracting crew arrived with building materials and packed lunches, and each evening, they returned on the barge back to the mainland. Charlie and Chelsea had gotten into the habit of running to the dock just before nine o'clock each morning to watch the barge arrive and following the crew back out at sunset to watch it disappear.

One morning, the kids were surprised to hear squeaky cries that grew louder as the barge approached. It sounded like a baby, but there were no babies on the island. They began to debate what could be making the sound.

"It's a rat!" shouted Chelsea. "See, I told you there were rats here," she teased, to which Charlie rolled his eyes.

"It's not a rat. It's a squirrel." Charlie looked more closely at the men as the barge docked and saw something wriggling in Jason's shirt. A blonde puffball with fuzzy ears stuck out from the top of his button down, and a tail wagged from the bottom.

"A puppy!" he shouted, running to greet the little animal with Chelsea at his heels. Jason pulled out a tiny golden retriever, no bigger than his hand. It was shivering and yelped louder when it saw the water around it, and Jason quickly stuffed the little animal back into his shirt.

The puppy had been sitting alone along the Harbor Marina dock just before they traveled over. With no collar, Jason had decided to take it with him until the owner of the missing animal came forward. Besides, he thought the kids could use a friend. They had not left the island since their arrival the week before, and he assumed that they were probably a little lonely.

"Can I hold him?" Charlie begged, as they approached the manor.

"Mom, look, a puppy!" Chelsea yelled, running into the house. Christina came outside to find Charlie carrying the little animal. Jason had told him to hold the puppy tightly so that it did not run off and get lost, and Charlie took those instructions seriously, holding it firmly across his chest.

"Who is this?" Christina asked with a smile. She had always loved animals and extended a hand to pet the puppy on the head.

"I found this little guy this morning on our way over," Jason explained. "I hope you don't mind him coming along with me for the day. I didn't want to just leave him by the shore."

"Of course not! I'm sure the kids will love having him here. But he has to stay outside, unless you want to be cleaning up after him all day," she said, glancing at the twins. They shook their heads. They did not want to clean up after him.

"Yuck!" exclaimed Charlie.

"There's some chicken wire in the basement. Chelsea, Charlie…you two can help me make a fence so that our little friend does not wander off. Give me a minute, though."

Christina and the men chatted about their projects for the day. The penthouse kitchen was nearly complete. The moldy ceiling had been carefully replaced with new drywall, which had been sanded and primed. Jason just needed to apply a final coat of paint to finish it up. Sam and Jeremy had been busily replacing the roof of the home given the nice weather the past few days and were almost finished. The next step was to replace all rotted wood around dormer windows so that no further leaks occurred. There was no use fixing up the house if water damage continued to deteriorate the inside. Christina looked forward to having use of the upstairs kitchen as the appliances were much nicer than those in the basement kitchen.

Christina and the children gathered the chicken wire, a hammer, wire cutters, and wood posts from the storage room in the basement and made their way out to the large grassy field beside the manor. Christina hammered down four posts into the soil, and the children helped to pull the chicken wire around the posts to create an enclosed fence for Ralphie, as they called the puppy. Christina clipped the wire and bent the ends through the loops to ensure that it was tight. It was not perfect, but would do the job until he learned to dig his way out. She placed water into one bowl and canned meat into another and left the kids and Ralphie, going back inside to work.

She spent the morning cleaning the manor's large windows. A darkness seemed to envelop the manor, even on the brightest days, and she suspected that a thorough cleaning was in order. Carrying a caddy with glass cleaner and rags, Christina moved room to room, diligently cleaning the dirt and grime from the windows until the rags were black with filth. By morning's end, the house smelled strongly of ammonia, and light fell in golden beams across the floor for the first time in years. But on the whole, the manor remained dreary and dark, as if the windows despised the light and sent it away.

Growing frustrated with the perpetual dimness that plagued the manor, she next decided to change out all of the light bulbs. Perhaps they were old or had low wattage. In either case, the problem was easy enough to remedy. After lunch, she worked diligently, dragging a ladder around with her as she replaced every light bulb in the house, forty-eight in all. Charlie was tasked with placing old light bulbs into the trash, while Chelsea supplied Christina with new ones. It was a system that sped up the tedious process but, nonetheless, took the better part of the afternoon.

After the final bulb was replaced, the kids excitedly ran out to check on Ralphie. They had heard little barks and squeals while they were working and were eager to play with their new friend. Christina was surprised to find them returning just as soon as they left.

"Mom!" they yelled in unison as they ran back towards the house. "Look what Ralphie did!"

Christina assumed that the puppy had pooped or perhaps chewed on the chicken wire or even scattered the food all around, but what she found left her shocked and perplexed. Ralphie was lying next to the food and water dishes, asleep and covered in dirt. The ground was covered with large, rectangular holes, spaced into neat rows and approximately one foot deep. Piles of dirt lied strewn about. Stranger still, the odd holes were not dug next to the fence, as one might expect, in an effort to escape.

"Did you do this?" she asked sternly of Charlie and Chelsea, knowing that they could not possibly have done it as they were with her the majority of the morning. But who else? Certainly not the tiny puppy. There was so much to do at the house, and the last thing she needed was to have projects added to her list. The twins shook their heads, annoyed at the insinuation.

"I told you, it was Ralphie," Charlie said, irritated that he was having to defend himself.

Christina picked up the little animal, who had, by then, awakened to their voices and was excitedly wagging his tail. His blonde fur and paws were filthy, and it was evident that he had been the digger of the holes. As she held him, she felt guilty for leaving him outside all day alone. How scary it must have been for him to be by himself and in a new place. If he returned Monday, she would make it a point to keep him company.

"Poor little guy. Why do you make big messes? Hmm?" She gave his belly a rub, and they played and took turns holding the puppy until the crew left for the weekend, taking him with them. As the men left, they recommended waiting to use the penthouse kitchen for one more day because of the strong paint fumes. They had left the windows open, though, and reminded Christina to close them should it rain.

It was getting close to dinner time, and the twins wanted macaroni and cheese, so Christina pulled out a pot from under the kitchen counter. She was used to eating children's meals, but in order to compromise, decided to make the meal from scratch. A radio sat on the countertop, which Christina had set to a station that played exclusively classical music. She turned it on as she often did when she cooked, and Andrea Bocelli's *Time to Say Goodbye* filled the silence with an aristocratic aura that she imagined once pervaded the home on a regular basis. She always felt as though her cooking improved with this music genre playing in the background and smiled at the perfection of her al dente pasta. If only John could see her cooking now, she thought, smiling at the irony.

Charlie and Chelsea sat down at the table, eagerly awaiting their meals. Still needing to add milk, butter, and cheeses, she walked to the fridge, sharing the twins' excitement for a real, home-cooked meal, but nearly jumped back in repulsion at what lied on the other side of the fridge door. The strong stench of rotting meat and produce smacked her in the face, powerfully enough to make her gag. All of the fresh food brought over by Mike the day before had rotted. The apples were brown and oozing fluid, the strawberries and cheeses molded, the meat browned and covered in maggots, and the milk curdled. Nothing was remotely edible. But the strangest thing of all was that the refrigerator appeared to be running normally. A cold stream of air poured out as the door stood open, and a gallon of juice sitting towards the back of the fridge had actually partially frozen. Christina quickly closed the fridge door and, not wanting to upset the children, served just pasta that night, explaining that she had forgotten to have Mike bring the cheese and milk. Charlie and Chelsea did not give her explanation of the meal change a second thought and, instead, babbled on about Ralphie and what they would do with him when he returned the following week.

But Christina sat, not touching her food. She could not stop thinking about the rotten groceries in the refrigerator. She had personally unloaded all of the food the day before and had actually mentioned to Mike how fresh the apples looked. Perhaps the refrigerator had stopped working for a few hours while no one was in the kitchen? But the decay of food would have taken more time than that. Perhaps the food only looked fresh but really wasn't? Whatever the case, they would need new food delivered. She hated to bother Mike on a weekend, but they desperately needed food, and he had offered to help out however needed. It was getting late, so she decided to call him first thing in the morning.

The three found themselves going to bed right after dinner. The change in light bulbs had done little to offset the perpetual dimness of the manor. It was quite difficult to read a book or even navigate around the house after the sun went down, and Christina decided she should add an electrician to the list of services needed in the manor. She would call Annette in the morning about it as well.

The children had moved to the second attic suite bedroom and shared the queen bed within it. They were happy to have a room to call their own, while Christina enjoyed not being kicked or pushed off the bed as she slept. But that evening, a familiar scream pierced the air. Christina ran to Chelsea's side, and held her tight until she awoke. The little girl cried as she frighteningly described a monster walking amongst the halls of the manor and watching her whilst she slept. Christina continued to hold her close and rubbed her back in an attempt to calm her.

"It was just a dream, sweetheart. See, I'm the only one here besides you and Charlie."

"No, Mama. There is someone else." She pointed towards the taxidermy room. "The man with red eyes," she whispered.

Christina started to reassure her that monsters are not real when she suddenly stopped mid-sentence and looked towards the door. There was a noise coming from the hallway, the unmistakable thump of footsteps. She listened for a moment longer, holding her breath, until the sound abruptly stopped. The hair on her arms stood straight up, and a surge of adrenaline made her heartbeat quicken. The silence was deafening. Then, the footsteps came again. Chelsea's eyes widened in terror. Christina struggled to hide her own fear as she tried to figure out what to do. She raised her index finger over her lips, silently pleading with Chelsea to remain quiet. Remembering that Charlie had brought a baseball bat with him, she quietly grabbed it from the closet and made her way towards the bedroom door, apprehensively peaking her head out. An empty hallway stood before her, no different than any other time she had seen it, and for a moment, she wondered whether there was anything wrong at all. But then there was movement. A large figure shifted around a corner and into eyesight. Fear ran through her, and she struggled to not scream out. It moved with heavy feet, its dark cloak sweeping the floor with each step, and a green, scaly, almost-human-looking hand hung by its side. It emitted a low-tone growl, like that of a wild dog, and the unmistakable smell of rotting meat. She stood paralyzed in fear.

Something clanked loudly against the floor. She looked down in horror, realizing that she had dropped the bat, and when she looked back, she was terrified to see that it was now watching her, its red eyes staring as if boring through her soul. It moved towards her, its footsteps shaking the wooden floor with each step.

In a moment of bravery, she picked up the bat and charged forward, swinging with every ounce of strength she had at the creature. A battle cry in the form of a loud, primal scream escaped from her lips. The creature suddenly vanished, nowhere to be seen, and she felt her body, devoid of energy, falling to the ground as she slipped into unconsciousness. For several minutes, there was only silence, until she awoke, gagging from the lingering smell of rot. But the hall stood empty, looking as innocent as any hallway. There was no creature, no cloak, nothing.

She stood stunned, not knowing what to do next. Had she, in her sleep-deprived and stressed state, compounded by Chelsea's recurrent nightmares, simply imagined the creature? Was she in need of psychological help? Or had she really seen something that defied explanation?

She decided it best to keep the mysterious event to herself. She did not want to scare the children and could not be certain that she had seen what she thought she had. She sat on the ground for a minute, took a few deep breaths, and walked back into the suite, where Chelsea sat nervously awaiting her return, still shaking with fright.

"Is it gone?" she asked.

"There's nothing you need to worry about," she assured her, pulling the covers back up over her small torso. She tucked in Chelsea's teddy as well. "It was probably just a small animal that made it into the house, but it's gone now." Even as the words came out of her mouth, she knew it was a lie.

"Then why did you scream?" she asked, not ready to accept Christina's explanation.

"Mommy saw a spider, but don't worry. I killed it," she said convincingly, hoping it was enough to settle her fears.

Chelsea accepted her explanation, appearing relieved, and after a lullaby, fell back asleep. Charlie had slept through the entire ordeal, and a puddle of drool was accumulating on his pillow. But Christina found it difficult to relax and did not sleep at all that night. She lied on the floor of the children's room with the baseball bat right beside her just in case the mysterious creature returned. But the rest of the night was quiet except for the sound of crickets chirping and cicadas buzzing outside. By morning, Christina had convinced herself that she had, most likely, experienced some sort of hallucination related to stress and fatigue and would bring it up at her yearly physical just to make sure she had not developed an underlying health condition.

Saturday morning, Mike awoke to the sound of his phone ringing. Annoyed, he checked the time. It was only eight o'clock.

"Who's that?" asked his wife groggily.

"I don't know, honey. Maybe it's Luke. Hello? Hello?"

"Your hearing aid," Cathy offered, handing Mike the device that he regularly took off at bedtime. He despised that hearing aid, as it served as a constant reminder of his advancing age.

"Hi, Mike. It's Christina…from the island. I'm sorry to bother you so early. Listen, we've had an issue with our groceries. It seems that all of the food has gone bad already, and we had to throw it all away. Would you possibly be able to bring us some new groceries? I have a list that I can text over."

"The groceries from Thursday?" he asked, perplexed.

"I'm not sure what happened, but everything seems to have spoiled, and now we have nothing to eat. I think the refrigerator is not working properly."

Mike was quiet for a moment as he recalled a similar experience that Bob had had with the refrigerator. He did not want to travel out to the island today. He had made plans to go golfing with his son. Saturday was the day that the two spent together, a tradition they had maintained since Luke was a little boy. But he had promised the family that he would be there to help and agreed to make a Saturday stop at the island.

Several hours later, the ferry arrived with an order nearly a duplicate of the one delivered just two days prior. As he and Christina walked back towards the ferry to gather more groceries, he suddenly stopped her. Looking back towards the house as he spoke, Christina picked up a sense of fear in his hushed voice, almost as if he thought he might be overhead.

"Listen, I don't mean to worry you, but I feel obligated to tell you something."

"Of course. What is it?" Christina asked, concerned, wondering what he could possibly have to tell her that required such secrecy.

"Annette's uncle, God rest his soul, lived for a time on the property while renovating, hoping to turn it into a bed and breakfast, I believe. I used to come up once a week and bring him groceries and what not. I remember him telling me that groceries I had brought not two days before suddenly all rotted, just like yours. At the time, I did not think much of it because he blamed it on the refrigerator malfunctioning, and I had no reason to question that, until I really got to thinking about it. It's just not possible for everything to go bad so quickly, fridge or no fridge."

"Well, our attic kitchen was just fixed up, so I plan to put these groceries up there."

"I only tell you this because I worry about you and the children staying in a place like this. Call me superstitious, but I've always sensed something strange about the home…the whole island, really. Things happen here that can't be explained. Just be careful."

"What do you mean?" Christina asked, her mind going back to the figure in the hallway. She felt a chill as she asked and probably would not have dared show any interest in such a topic had it not been brought up by someone else first.

Mike, on the other hand, seemed far less apprehensive to discuss the matter. "My childhood friend, Albert, worked with Jason and Jeremy on the manor when Bob lived here. They had worked together for a long time before that and never had any problems with each other. Albert was a good, honest man and loved his work, and gosh was he good at it too. Give him a task, and consider it done. He was especially good with the old plumbing." He looked at the ground, taking in a breath and holding it for a few seconds before continuing. "At first, he really liked coming out to the island. Thought it was a gem being so close to the Hamptons while feeling like you were out in nature. But slowly, he began to change. He became more reclusive and developed a dread for working in the manor. He stopped wanting to talk to anyone…even me, his closest friend. Then, one day, I got a call from Jeremy asking if I had heard anything from Albert. Apparently, he was acting off after leaving the island one afternoon and announced, out of the blue, that he was quitting. I called him right away, and he sounded paranoid, like he was scared of something out here. He never told me what happened that day, but I imagine it must have been something horrible. And that was the last time I spoke to him. No one knows where he went off to. Knew him for fifty years, and he just disappeared."

"I'm sorry to hear about that," she said. "I imagine that was difficult for you to lose someone you knew so long."

"It's not been easy, especially not knowing what happened to him. And then poor Bob died so suddenly out here. I'm telling you, there's something going on. I just can't quite put my finger on it. Just keep a close watch on the kids…and be careful yourself," he cautioned.

Christina listened, surprised to learn that Annette's uncle had died on the property. "Yeah, how sad. Bob had a heart attack, didn't he?" It was something she had not asked Annette because she did not want to pry but had assumed, given the sudden nature of his passing. She felt that Annette would have discussed it more with her if she was comfortable doing so.

Mike looked surprised. "No, it wasn't a heart attack." He hesitated, and Christina worried she had prodded too much, yet she suddenly felt a strong need to learn what happened to him.

"Please tell me what happened," she begged.

"I don't think Annette would want it getting out, so keep it between you and me. Bob hung himself from one of the rafters in the church. I'm sorry to have to be the one to tell you that."

Christina was unprepared for what she heard. "My God. I had no idea. How sad for Annette." She, once again, scolded herself for not having checked in on Annette more often these past few months. But at the same time, she felt a little irritated that she had not been made aware of a suicide taking place where she had brought her children to live. "Does anyone know why?"

"Rumor around town has it that a suicide note was left behind. He mentioned hearing voices in his head that told him to hurt himself and made it impossible to sleep. It seems he felt he had no way out. His death was his third suicide attempt, apparently."

Just then, the twins wandered over, wanting to see the ferry before it left, and their conversation came to an abrupt end. Mike's news was unsettling, especially given the events of the night before, and Christina began to wonder what she had signed up for. It was becoming clear that she had not been given the full story of Statham

Island, and she somewhat resented the lack of transparency on Annette's end. For the first time since her separation from John, she found herself missing a partner to confide in.

She sent the kids off to start chores. It was Charlie's job to fold laundry and Chelsea's to put away clean dishes that had been set out on a cloth to dry. Meanwhile, she headed up to the church, more curious about it now that she knew its dark history. She hesitated for a moment at the dog pen, its holes an eyesore, and looked at the innocent-looking stone structure before her. A cloud of mystery and sadness seemed to encompass it now. Curiosity pulled her closer, despite the smell of rot, which, once confined to the inside of the building, permeated the outside as if warning potential visitors to stay back. Ignoring a primal urge to return to the manor, she walked up to the double doors, pulling them wide open. Within were empty pews, waiting for the churchgoers who would never come. Large wooden beams supported the ceiling and walls, like one might find in a centuries-old English home. Was it from one of the beams that Bob had hung himself, she morbidly pondered. The knowledge that Bob had died within that space made it impossible to think of anything else, and she understood why Annette wanted to tear it down.

As she turned to leave, something on the altar caught her attention. It was shiny, highlighted by a single beam of sunlight that flowed through the building's rear stained glass window. She moved closer, curious, and had the terrible sensation of a hundred unseen eyes upon her, watching her every move. She reached out for a moment, not knowing what it was, and then realized, shocked, that the object was something very familiar to her…her grandmother's wedding ring. There was no mistaking it. The center diamond surrounded by eight rubies had been hers since her grandmother's death and was always kept locked in a safe. She had placed it in the manor's cigar room safe herself, diligently locking it up just a day prior. She had even triple-checked that the door was locked tight. There was no logical explanation for how it could have made its way outside. She grabbed the ring and put it on her ring finger for safe keeping as she quickly exited the chapel, hardly needing to assist the doors as they slammed shut with a reverberating bang. The negativity surrounding the building created a thickness in the air that seemed to, almost physically, push her away.

She sprinted back to the manor, and when she got inside, found that the twins had diligently completed their chores. The laundry sat loosely folded in a basket at the foot of the basement stairs, and all of the dishes had been put away into the cupboards. The kids sat quietly at the table, eating a snack, oblivious to anything that had just transpired.

"Hey, you two. Did either of you get into the safe?"

They both shook their heads.

"I found this ring in the chapel. Are you sure you didn't take it to play with? I'm not mad. I just want to know how you figured out the code." The code she had set was the date she had graduated from law school, a date neither had any knowledge of, and she wondered whether the lock had somehow broken.

Again, they both denied any involvement in the ring's disappearance or playing around the chapel.

"You told us not to go there," Charlie replied.

"Yes, but someone put the ring there."

"Well, it wasn't us," Chelsea insisted.

Christina decided to drop it. She could tell when the twins were lying, and they certainly were not lying now. She checked the manor's safe and found it locked, just as she had left it. The rest of her jewelry sat exactly as she had placed it, still stacked in order, and it now seemed silly to have blamed the children for the missing ring. She began to wonder whether it could have been someone on the construction crew. They had worked in the manor before. Perhaps they knew about the safe and were able to pick the lock. But why would they leave such a valuable piece just sitting on the altar? And why was nothing else missing? Her wedding ring from John had a much larger diamond and was still there, as were a tennis bracelet and several gold earrings. If someone was committing robbery, why just take one item? And she had a good sense about people. She felt that the men were trustworthy and would not have done something of that nature.

But if not them, then who? A far more sinister thought crossed her mind as she recalled the events of the night before. She vaguely remembered the figure's hand clasped tightly around something. Had it been the ring? How ridiculous. She reminded herself that she, in her tired state, had probably just imagined the entirety of what was witnessed, an explanation she would continue to fall back on each time her mind wandered back to that night, almost as a survival mechanism, because the alternative was far too horrid to even consider.

Monday morning, Charlie and Chelsea ran out to meet the construction crew as usual, and much to their joy, the puppy returned with them. But Christina lied in bed. She felt as though she was coming down with something. Her limbs felt weak, and she had no appetite. Mustering all of her energy, she donned a robe and went downstairs to talk to the men, keeping a distance in case she had some contagious illness.

"Come here, Ralphie!" Charlie beckoned the little puppy, who leaped from Jason's arms and into his, wagging his tail and eager to play.

"Just keep him outside," Christina reminded him and gave him a gentle pat. She looked at Jason and Jeremy. "How was your weekend?" She was surprised to find that Sam was not amongst them. "Where's Sam?"

"Oh, his truck wasn't working this morning. He told us he'd be in after he got it fixed." Jeremy smiled. His kids were about the same age as the twins and had spent the weekend playing with the puppy. "Hey, how about you two put Ralphie in the pen and then help me carry in some paint cans." They jumped with excitement at the thought of being able to assist and quickly left with the puppy. There was scraping and painting that needed to be done on the windows and doors. The men had also brought two new front doors and scaffolding along.

Jason stayed behind. "Hey, Chelsea just told me that someone "scary" was in your home. Is that right? Did someone break in?" He imagined that the water surrounding the property would be a huge deterrent to burglars and hoped that it was just a story she had made up.

"Well, she's been getting these nightmares that she thinks are real…and it was just one of those."

"Oh, that's a relief. She had me convinced," he said with a laugh. "I mean, I'm sorry that she's having nightmares, but I'm glad that's all it was." He mentioned that he, too, had recurrent nightmares as a child that kept his parents up at night but, much to their relief, finally grew out of them.

But as he spoke, tears began to well up in Christina's eyes. *Stop it*, she told herself. *It was a figment of your imagination.* But she knew it was not. She had told no one of what she saw or that she had not slept in days because the thought of it possibly returning was overwhelming. For the first time in her life, she feared for her and the kids' safety in a way that she had never even experienced in the city. Every sound terrified her, and every abnormal smell invoked a sense of dread. Would this creature return? Was it there all the time?

Would it hurt them? Unable to hold it in any longer, she heard words flowing from her mouth that she had vowed to keep to herself.

"Actually, there may have been someone. I saw something…somebody in the hallway the other night. Maybe a person living on the island and breaking in?" She confessed that she was afraid to be living alone with two little kids, not knowing whether the intruder would return. She could not bring herself to admit that she questioned whether it was human at all. Despite not knowing Jason well, she instinctually trusted him and found great comfort in the fact that he was simply willing to listen.

Jason remembered an incident with Albert years before when the crew was helping Bob with renovations. Albert had shared with him that he had been working on a broken pipe in the basement kitchen when he supposedly saw a man walk past him. He had only mentioned it after several of his tools went missing, and he wanted to know where they were. But Jason had not taken them, and Jeremy had not even been at the property that day. After that, Albert seemed to change. He became more distant and more easily agitated in the weeks leading up to his disappearance. Jason suspected that something had affected him so deeply, so negatively, at the manor that he left his job, his acquaintances, and his entire life behind, never to return. He refrained from mentioning any of this to Christina. He did not want to scare her with stories that most likely had no connection.

"If it makes you feel better, I am happy to stay here with you and the kids so that you don't have to be alone, as long as you don't mind Ralphie staying, too. Just until we figure out what is going on around here, I can stay in one of the guest rooms on the second floor, and honestly, you'd get more work out of me," he joked. "Obviously, Jeremy and Sam need to go home to their families, but hopefully, I can take a little stress off your plate."

Under normal circumstances, Christina would have found herself saying that she was okay and thanking the person for offering. She was used to being an independent woman and, especially of late, not relying upon others. But she was desperate for someone to step into the situation and help. Jason decided to move in the following day, which meant only one more night alone on the island, and it was the best piece of news Christina had had in a long time.

Chapter Five

The setting sun cast rays of red, orange, and yellow that danced along the waves of the incoming tide. A chorus of cicadas and a night owl, and the intermittent flapping of wings as bats descended and then quickly ascended back into the sky, created a natural orchestra that one might never know existed if not for an occasional escape from traffic and the big city. It was the hiatus from life that Christina had been promised by Annette and so desperately needed. One might even call it a rejuvenation of the soul.

Chelsea and Charlie were spending the week with John and Rachel. He had suddenly taken interest in a family trip to Disney World, and Christina had reluctantly agreed to let them go. Perhaps a break in schedule would reset Chelsea's sleep cycle and rid her of the horrendous nightmares that continued to plague the family on a nightly basis. At the very least, she would have more time to devote to gardening and catching up on rest. She had waved goodbye to the twins as Mike pulled away from the shore and cried when John texted her fifteen minutes later to let her know that they were in his car and on their way to the airport. But they would be back in a week, she told herself.

She and Jason made it a habit to sit together along the south shore of the island every evening after dinner. They would bring wine, cheese, and blankets and sit for hours, Ralphie by their side, just talking. Jason liked to share jokes that he came across, and Christina laughed harder than she remembered in years. Jason's presence brought her out of a deep hole of despair and back into reality. Gone was the constant fear she felt in the days prior to him moving in. She was sleeping better and felt a renewed motivation to restore the manor to its former grandeur. She had removed the encroaching ivy growing along the front of the home and single-handedly trimmed all of the bushes on the property, which was no small feat and had left her body bloodied and aching, reminding her, lest she forget, that she was not as young as she used to be. The crew had supplied a riding lawnmower, which would stay on the property until renovations were complete, and her next task was to tackle the overgrown lawns, which consisted largely of weeds and tree sprouts, rather than grass.

"So, what made you and Jeremy decide to go into construction?"

Jason took a swig from a joint and handed it over to Christina.

"Before our dad passed, he was a home inspector. We used to go around with him to different houses, you know, just for the fun of it. And when he got sick, we needed extra money, so we worked for a contracting company in Anchorage and learned how to build. I think it's safe to say we both have a love for turning a pile of wood into something beautiful."

Christina smiled, as that was exactly how she felt about renovating. Turning something old into something new was also a shared passion between her and Annette, and working on home improvement projects together had sealed their friendship.

"You used to be an attorney, right?" Christina had not been in the Hamptons long, but already, the rumors around town had started swirling. According to Annette, everyone wanted to know about the new family living on the mysterious island. "What brought you all the way out here?"

Over the past few months, she had expected someone to ask the dreaded question and had prepared herself to avoid spilling the dirty details of her marriage's collapse in a manner that would drive others away. It was one thing to talk to Annette but quite another to discuss details with someone who knew very little, possibly nothing, of what had transpired.

"Yes," she confirmed, handing back the joint, "but I'm taking a break after a rather awful divorce. Annette took pity on me and offered to let me live out here and oversee renovations while I…recuperate, I guess you could call it." It sounded polished and classy and was not the Jerry Springer *my husband cheated on me and knocked up another woman* reply that she feared may someday find its way out.

"How did the kids handle that?" Jason asked, silently wondering whether Chelsea's dreams were a product of the marriage's dissolution. He had grown fond of the children and could only imagine that it had been trying on them, especially given their age. Charlie took it the hardest, but they are both adapting as well as they can. No one comes out of these things unscathed, you know." It was evident as she spoke that despite her strength, the divorce had taken a piece out of her, too.

Her mind wandered back to the events of the past year. One minute, her marriage seemed solid. She and John each had their respective careers and enjoyed spending time together as a family. Last summer, she never could have imagined being divorced, much less John having started a whole new life with someone else. If someone had told her it would happen, she would have thought they were joking. Their marriage, like any, had ups and downs, but far more good times than bad. They enjoyed each other's company and fought very little.

They had met in their early twenties while John was still in the Air Force. He had taken a nasty spill while biking with some friends. Christina, at the time, was a young nurse at the local medical center and had helped to dress his wounds. She had long hair at the time, which she wore pulled back into a ponytail, revealing a soft face and bright green eyes that drew him in. He had asked her to a steakhouse for dinner, and soon after, the couple was spending every free moment together.

A few months later, Christina found herself rushing to the hospital after her brother, Nick, was admitted with sepsis. He spent a week on the ventilator and suffered damage to multiple organs before miraculously making a full recovery. The doctors were stunned by how quickly his health returned and cautioned him to avoid eating any more undercooked shellfish in the future. Vibrio vulnificus is what they called it. Nick promised to avoid the offending food and was eager to get home but, sadly, would never leave the hospital. A physician error resulted in him receiving a medication he was allergic to, and despite several doses of epinephrine, he passed away the following day of anaphylactic shock. Christina had never been able to recover from his death and went into a deep depression. She could no longer treat her own patients without seeing the face of her brother, and on more than one occasion, found herself locked in a bathroom stall, crying, and unable to perform her job duties. She walked away from the healthcare field altogether, and months later, found herself taking pre-law classes and studying for the LSATs as her desire to help patients now came in the form of medical malpractice lawsuits.

Throughout their marriage, Christina and John had pushed each other to be the best in their respective fields. Christina became a top-notch attorney representing victims of medical malpractice, while John advanced as a pilot, eventually working for a commercial airline. It completely caught her by surprise when a close friend, who worked as a flight attendant and often shared flights with John, told her that she suspected he was having an affair with a fellow flight attendant named Rachel. Crew members often spent layovers together, and she was privy to much of their activity. She had noticed an inappropriate closeness between the two that had crossed the boundaries of professionalism. There was the time in Frankfurt when John gave her his coat on a chilly day, despite Rachel having her own, and then put his arm around her. She saw how Rachel gawked at John whenever he told one of his stories about a horrible passenger or a difficult landing. The last straw was when she saw Rachel leave his hotel room early one morning wearing nothing but his button-down shirt. Christina was in utter disbelief at the news and in denial until she mustered up the courage to review his credit card transactions. There, she found charges for expensive jewelry, fancy dinners, and concert tickets, none of which had been for her, the evidence of which she aptly saved and later filed in her divorce proceedings.

"I'm sure that was tough on them…and you," Jason offered, bringing her out of deep thought.

Christina nodded, raising her eyebrows. "Yeah, you could say that. Well, come on, what's your story?" Jason looked out towards the water. It was a question that he dreaded, the kind that brought an instant pain to his heart and served as a reminder of what could have been. He rolled the joint between his fingers anxiously, hesitating in his response.

"I was married, about fifteen years ago, to a sweet lady named Nikki. We met a few years after I moved to New York. I was working hard with Jeremy on getting the company up and running, and she was a nanny for one of the wealthy families in town who had hired us to redo their basement. We hit it off right away, and I knew she was the one. Three months later, we were married. We were really happy." He paused for a moment. "About a year after we got married, I was busy working on a renovation when I got a call from the hospital, asking if I was her husband. She had been in a car accident, but they wouldn't tell me any more until I got there.

So I rushed over to Stony Brook to see her. She was in a coma for two weeks before she passed. She was eight months pregnant, and we lost our baby boy, too. In an instant, my life was changed. I kind of lost myself after that. I struggled with alcohol for a while and only found stability again when I put all of my focus into work. Without Jeremy, I don't know what I would have done. But life goes on, whether we want it to or not." He had told his story to only a few people because life seemed easier when he pretended it had not happened. But despite his stoic front and the absence of tears, Christina could sense the enormity of the burden he carried.

"I'm so sorry. I had no idea." She, herself, had lost two pregnancies while going through IVF and understood the permanent pain inflicted by the loss of a child. Christina put her arm around him, and the two sat silently until the sun finally went down, breathing in the saltiness of the air and allowing nature and human connection to heal the deepest of wounds.

The following day, Christina and Jason took a much-needed break from their work and traveled into town. Sam and Jeremy were busy working on the house when they left and would not need the barge until later that day. It was the first time Christina had returned to the mainland since renovations began, and despite the island's vastness, she was starting to get cabin fever. The two climbed aboard the barge, a couple piles of lumbar still resting along the railing base, and headed towards East Hampton for the day. Jeremy watched from the dock, holding Ralphie. His kids had begged to keep him, and since no one had posted any missing puppy fliers, Jeremy agreed, buying him a little collar with a bone pendant engraved with his name.

Across the water sat Donna, the car, just where Christina had left it weeks earlier. It looked dirty, and someone had obviously banged their car door into hers. A small dent sat just beside the keyhole, and she groaned when she realized no one had left a note on her windshield. Typical New Yorkers, she thought to herself.

The two spent the morning visiting the historic Mulford Farm. The seventeenth-century museum had been a destination that she and John had always planned to visit on their trips to the area, but they had never found the time to fit it in. The wooden, colonial structure sat strongly and proudly, a testament to the building skills of past generations. It was a home that Jason had often admired, himself, for that reason.

The two wandered along Main Street, stopping at small boutiques. Christina picked up some scented candles, hoping to help the manor feel a little more welcoming. She also needed a few toiletries, which she purchased at a corner pharmacy. After enjoying a lunch of lobster and crabs, the two drove to Cedar Point County Park, a few miles away, and spent the afternoon biking trails around the six-hundred-acre property, taking in the beautiful views of the bay. By the end of the ride, both laughed as they searched each other for ticks, heeding the warnings of other bikers in the area.

It felt rejuvenating to treat herself after months of gloominess. It was as if the warm sun had finally peaked out from the clouds after a long, cold winter. She smiled to herself, thankful that happiness still existed…and thankful for having found Jason. He held her hand and pulled her closer, and she felt an energy run through her body as his lips pressed against her own. Despite the park being quite crowded, it was, even if for a brief moment, just the two of them in their own little bubble, impervious to the world around them.

A corner of Jason's mouth yielded a smile, and she could not help but smile back. Finding a new relationship had not been a priority, but here it was, as if the world had seen her plight and responded with mercy. She had not known him long, but something told her she had found the one, and if she had learned anything over the years, it was to trust her gut.

They returned their bikes and walked hand-in-hand back to Donna. By the time they reached the barge, both were physically exhausted and ready to relax for the evening. They had walked and biked nearly the entire day. And as the barge docked back at Statham Island, both wanted nothing more than to shower and slide into comfortable pajamas for the evening. Sam and Jeremy were waiting on the dock with Ralphie, eager to get home to their respective families, and left after a quick greeting.

Light emanated from the windows of Statham Manor as if awaiting guests, its beauty becoming more striking with each day of repairs. The two were busy discussing what to make for dinner when Jason suddenly stopped in his tracks. There was the sound of something heavy falling inside. He had been on high alert around the property ever since Christina mentioned possibly seeing someone in the house. But mental preparations for possibly encountering someone uninvited did not lesson the shock of seeing a dark figure move past an upstairs window. The two stood frozen in their footsteps, too stunned to move, and Christina audibly gasped as the figure walked past the window a second time.

"You see that, right?" she whispered.

"We need to call the police." Not taking his eyes off the window, Jason reached into his back pocket, pulling out his phone.

Christina felt relieved that she was not the only one witnessing the intruder. It was an attestation to her sanity. She was glad the children were with John and shuddered to think of them being at the manor with this intruder wandering the halls.

The two backed away from the house, taking care to move silently towards the tree line, where they waited for nearly forty-five minutes for a police boat to arrive. Four policemen with flashlights in hand introduced themselves by name and asked what was going on. Jason explained the history of a trespasser, who seemed to have returned.

"We'll take a look," a man with a badge reading Officer Murphy replied. Christina handed over her keys, pointing out a gold key that unlocked the padlock on the taxidermy room door, just in case it was needed. He motioned to his partner to follow, while the other two officers remained behind to take a statement.

The men walked room to room, guns drawn, clearing each section until the manor had been scoured thoroughly. There was no intruder to be found, but it was evident that someone had indeed been in the home. It looked as though a tornado had made its way through the manor. Furniture in several rooms had been moved and overturned, paintings had been knocked off of walls, and glassware from the kitchen lied shattered across the stone floor. Strangely enough, nothing appeared to be missing, and even the safe in the cigar room remained locked. A platter and candle holders made of silver sat in plain view, albeit knocked over. Two bedrooms upstairs had been ransacked, yet again, items seemingly of high value, including a large collection of original nineteenth-century oil paintings, had been left behind, mystifying the responding officers. And most baffling of all was the stack of books left on the second-floor hallway, which presumably had come from the library. A collection of thirty-seven books were piled neatly, one on top of the other. It looked as though a simple poke would knock the entire stack down. Why would an intruder take the time to do that? It was a thought that disturbed them to the core, especially the older of the two gentlemen, Officer Malcolm, who exited the manor as quickly as professionally possible.

Christina and Jason were shocked to learn of the state of the manor but found little comfort in the fact that the trespasser had left the manor. The island was large and had many areas in which one could hide and wait. The thought that this person was still around, somewhere unseen, seemed nearly as frightening as having him in the house.

It was dark, hindering the ability of the officers to search the property thoroughly. With flashlights, Officers Aubrey and Dunce walked the perimeter of the island, looking for any signs of abnormality, but found none. No tents, no fire pits, and no visible foot prints. It was as if everything on the island was normal, except that it wasn't. They could feel eyes upon them, watching their every move, yet they could see only darkness.

At the end of an exhaustive search, Christina realized that no one had searched the church. The thought crossed her mind that this intruder may have been the one responsible for taking her grandmother's ring, and if so, could very well be utilizing the chapel as a hideout. She ran over to the officers, informing them of her suspicions, and the officers wasted no time heading for the double doors, guns drawn and prepared to encounter the sly prowler. But after only a few moments, an "all clear" could be heard from the building, followed by the officers quickly reemerging, gagging. A sickening smell escaped from the doors, the unmistakable scent of rot and decay, one that reminded Officer Murphy of walking into a home where a corpse had lied for days before discovery.

And then, around the back of the church, movement. The officers, still recovering from the overpowering smell of death, shone their flashlights in the direction of movement. "Stop, police!" Officer Aubrey yelled. His voice seemed to echo for a moment and was followed by silence. Everything around them stood still, as if time had stopped. Not even the leaves moved in the breeze, and the sound of the crickets ceased. There were no footsteps…nothing.

The officers quickly ran towards the movement, spotting the shadowy figure once more before it seemingly vanished into the tree line. The wooded area contained significant underbrush and branches that should have yielded sounds of footsteps, but again, nothing. The officers searched fruitlessly until they were eventually forced to call it a night.

Their departure brought no comfort to Jason and Christina, who were left with a manor in disarray on an island harboring a trespasser. The two worked until around two o'clock in the morning, picking up furniture and sweeping up glass, and Jason walked the home twice, ensuring windows and doors were locked before both finally fell asleep for the night. The feeling of an acute threat dissipated as morning approached, but the fear of who...or what...had invaded the home remained.

Jeremy and Sam arrived early the next morning with Ralphie in tow. The puppy was becoming more interested in exploring his surroundings and less easily restrained within the confines of the pen. He would whine and bark incessantly during the day, to the point that the crew was starting to feel guilty about leaving him there. But today, Sam brought several toys for Ralphie to play with...a ball, a couple of rope toys, some chewing bones, and even deluxe dog food...hoping to keep the little one occupied while they refinished the hardwoods.

Christina had planned to score the walls and begin the tedious process of removing wallpaper but, unfortunately, had awoken feeling drained and weak. It was hard to imagine that, just yesterday, she had walked and ridden a bike around East Hampton, and she hoped she had not caught a virus while in town. The thought crossed her mind that perhaps her fatigue was due to her rapidly approaching middle age and that the exercise was simply leaving her sore. She had no appetite but carried around a cup of coffee, still in her pajamas. Christina no longer cared that the crew might see her in that state and had grown comfortable having them around. Her pajama top hung loosely from her body, and she wondered whether she had lost more weight.

She offered to take Ralphie to the pen and gently plucked him from Sam's arms. Inside the confines of the chicken wire were a few toys that the kids had willingly given to the puppy. An old soccer ball sat in the far corner, and a few stuffed animals, now wet from the recent rains and covered in mud, lied scattered about. As she spread out the new toys and food from Sam, she noticed something peculiar. Each of the holes dug by Ralphie had become deeper by about six inches and appeared to be of wider breadth. She exercised caution to avoid falling in and spraining an ankle and hoped that the toys would act as a distraction from the constant digging that was obviously occurring.

Suddenly, there was the unmistakable, overpowering feeling of being watched. She looked behind her, instinctively towards the chapel, but saw nothing before turning in a three-hundred-sixty-degree circle, quickly scanning every bush and tree for the slightest bit of movement, yet everything appeared as it should. But still, something felt dangerous, and the hairs on her arms stood straight up. She grabbed the handle of a hiking knife that sat hidden in her pocket, scanning the tree line once again, but released its grip after a moment. Nothing appeared out of the ordinary. There were no footsteps…only the sound of leaves rustling as the wind brushed by.

Ralphie seemed immersed in his new toys, and she returned to the manor, hoping that a little bit of food would help her to feel better. Plastic hung from the ceiling of the foyer and stairs, and the men could be heard talking in the next room as she made her way up to the second-floor hallway. She wanted to first examine the strange stack of books before clearing them away. In the commotion of the evening, she had not been able to look at them and had grown curious as to why an intruder would take the time to go through the library and pile books so neatly.

The stack, consisting of alphabetized volumes belonging to several different leather-bound encyclopedia collections, stood several feet tall and had already been scooted to the side of the hallway. She could tell that no fingerprints had been taken by the lack of powder residue on their bindings. The books were circa 1960 and still in pristine condition. The pages were free of markings and had obviously been used very little, perhaps even as filler for the library shelves. Bundle by bundle, she carried the books back to the library, placing them on an empty shelf sitting just above eye level. To her dismay, the mystery of why the books had been moved remained.

In the kitchen, she ate half of the cheerios she had poured for herself and sipped hot coffee, unable to think about anything other than the night prior. She had called Annette right after the police left. Annette had apologized profusely for the break-in and even offered to come and stay with her, but Christina had declined given that Jason was now living at the manor. Annette was surprised to learn how close their friendship had grown but did not mind, happy that Christina seemed to be moving on from her broken marriage.

"So, are you two dating?" she asked, curious as to how serious the relationship actually was and what she had been missing while away from the island.

"I think so," Christina replied, excitedly thinking back to the kiss at the park, although the two had not had a chance to discuss what they were given the commotion of the night before.

"Have you guys…"

"Stop being so nosy," Christina giggled. "He's cute…and so good with the kids. He brought them a puppy to play with, too. Don't worry, he stays outside."

"Oh, my goodness! Well, he sounds like a keeper. I'm happy for you. But as a friend, I feel obligated to remind you to just be careful. Make sure he's really everything you think he is before it gets too serious."

"I know. I know," Christina replied with an unseen eye roll, a little annoyed that she would question her judgment.

"Otherwise, he'll have me to deal with," Annette laughed.

While Sam and the brothers busily moved the furniture on the second floor down to the first floor in preparation for sanding, Christina began to score the wallpaper in the living room. It seemed the logical place to start as it was out of the way of the sanding and an eyesore that she was eager to remedy and cross off the list. The wallpaper choice had obviously been expensive when it was purchased and retained a beautiful texture to its floral pattern, despite having yellowed with age and torn in several places. In one area of the room, wide strips hung off the wall, begging to be pulled, yet the thick and uneven texture of it made removal difficult.

The walls were soaked with a homemade mixture of fabric softener and water. Then began the tedious work of scraping, yielding only dime-sized scraps of wallpaper at a time, and after a good hour, she was beginning to regret having taken it on. She was not feeling any better than she had early that morning, and after checking briefly on Ralphie, who still seemed content with his new toys, she laid on the sofa for a power nap. It was rare that she afforded herself the luxury of naps, always finding excuses to push through whatever it was she happened to be focused on at the moment. But today was different. She had no choice in the matter and fell asleep within minutes, her eyes heavy with drowsiness and limbs weak with fatigue, and began to dream about the night before. As if observing through a one-way window, she could see a figure roaming the library, collecting books, and carrying them to the second floor. She watched as it stacked the books, seemingly in an organized fashion, rearranging every so often until satisfied. The alphabetic letters on each book spine glowed a neon green that would, at times, disappear and then reappear, sometimes pulsating, as if the books had a life of their own. She wondered whether the letters bore some significance.

The sound of Ralphie's barks awakened her. She had to look at the books and grabbed her phone, scrolling to the picture she had taken of the book stack the night before. Several photographs, including those of the books and the tossed furniture, had been sent to Annette in case she needed to make an insurance claim. Christina counted twenty-seven books, each of which displayed a categorical letter. She tilted the phone, then tilted it back, wondering what it could mean, if anything. And then it suddenly made sense. The letters seemed to jump out at her, just as they had in her dream. When read in order from top to bottom, they clearly spelled out:

LEAVEBEFOREITSTOOLATEGETOUT. She reread the message several times, but there was no mistaking it. *Leave before it's too late. Get out!*

She nearly dropped her phone. A cold chill ran down her back and the hairs stood on her arms.

"Jason!" she yelled, running towards the sound of sanding upstairs. "Jason!" she yelled louder. Jeremy and Sam were busy working, but Jason was nowhere to be found. "Where's Jason?" she asked the two men. She did not want to tell them what she had deciphered as she did not think they would believe her. She really wasn't sure if Jason would believe her either, but she at least knew he would listen.

"He just went to take care of Ralphie," Sam replied, and she ran out the door, eager to share with him what she had discovered, whether or not he found it notable.

Jason was holding the puppy outside of the pen, rocking him slowly, and it was clear that something was wrong. Running up to them, Christina was shocked to find his paws bloodied and the puppy shaking.

"Oh gosh! What happened?"

"I'm not sure. I found him barking and digging this," he said with a concerned expression, pointing to the ever-expanding holes in the ground. "Look at his paws," he said, holding a bloodied paw out for her to witness.

"Poor thing. Why do you think he's digging like this?" Christina asked.

"I don't know," Jason said matter-of-factly. He looked concerned, but she did not know him well enough to decipher what he was thinking.

A sense of guilt set in, and Christina regretted not having gone to check on Ralphie when she heard him barking. But then again, she had no reason to believe anything was wrong. "Let's take him in and clean him up. Come here, baby," she said, reaching for the little dog.

She prepared a bubble bath in the kitchen sink, where she bathed the puppy in warm water. He splashed around, seeming to forget about his injuries.

"There's something very wrong going on here," Christina finally said after a few minutes of silence. "Those holes keep getting bigger, and it's freaking me out that they're in perfect little rows. They almost look like graves."

"You don't think there are graves there, do you? There's no way something like that would have gone unnoticed all these years," Jason continued.

"I need to show you something." She hesitated for a moment, afraid of sounding paranoid. She showed Jason the picture of the bookstack. "What do you see here?"

"Books in the hallway."

"Look closer," Christina instructed, zooming into the letters along the book spines.

"I don't know. They're out of order."

Christina gave him a playful slap on the shoulder. "No, what do the letters spell?"

A few seconds passed as he deciphered the apparent message. "Did you do that?" he asked in a serious tone.

"Of course not!" Christina was annoyed he would even suggest that.

Jason agreed that it was strange and felt a renewed angst that the trespasser had yet to be found. It reminded him of why he chose to stay at the manor, and he felt ready to guard her should the person return.

Later that afternoon, they moved the puppy pen up to the front of the house, next to the brick drive. There, they could keep a better eye on Ralphie as they worked and hear him if he was upset. The holes were refilled with dirt, and the land, despite missing patches of grass, regained a somewhat normal appearance.

The crew left early, and Christina and Jason wandered back to the small, private beach, hand in hand. This time, they took Ralphie with them. They sat there for some time, talking and eating blueberries that grew along the edge of the sand and woods. They marveled at how big the puppy was getting. Its golden fur was transitioning from a baby chicken yellow to a deep golden color.

Jason mentioned that Sam and Jeremy planned to ask around town whether anyone else had experienced break-ins. And for the first time since coming back to the island, they talked about the kiss.

"So, are we a couple now?" Jason asked, pulling her in for a hug.

"If you're willing to put up with me, then I guess so," Christina joked.

It felt good to be wanted again. For so long now, Christina had felt like a favorite old sweater that had finally been donated to the thrift shop. In the darkest of months following John's leaving, she had never expected to find love again. Yet someone had found her and appreciated her for who she was.

Without the kids there, they were soaking up as much time together as they could. Christina sat in front of Jason, his arms wrapped around her as they talked, careful to not ruin the moment with discussions of what had happened the night before. The crashing waves were becoming stronger, and thunder and lightning were moving in. Christina leaned back for a final kiss before they headed back to the house. A loud, thunderous clap rang from above, and they scurried back inside, narrowly escaping a torrential downpour. They fell asleep in Christina's bed, lying side by side, with Ralphie on a pillow between them.

Chapter Six

Any desire to finish removing the wallpaper was lost after Sam offered to sand the walls, which he promised to be a much more efficient use of time. She decided to let him take on the project, as the men were ahead of schedule with the floors. An initial coat of polyurethane had been laid upstairs, and the second coat could not be applied until the following day. Jason and Jeremy barely missed Sam as they busied themselves sanding the first floor.

Christina donned rubber boots and garden gloves as she had a special project in mind for the day. It was a surprise for the kids. She did not think that Annette would mind, and it may even be a selling point for a potential buyer. But for the time being, it would be Charlie and Chelsea's.

Returning to the basement storage room, she found several wood stakes, which she carried outside to an area near the old greenhouse. The day prior, Mike had delivered groceries and a couple other supplies, including mesh netting and tomato, pepper, and strawberry plants that she had asked him to bring. He had also brought five peonies of various colors as a gift, which she was delighted to receive and would add to the garden. It was nearly midsummer and too late to start growing from seeds.

Christina wrapped the mesh around the posts, reminiscent of the pen she made for Ralphie, and worked hard to clear the land of leaves and weeds. She tilled the soil and divided the garden into sections for tomatoes, peppers, strawberries, and flowers. The plants appeared healthy and strong, and after planting the final plant, she took a step back and proudly examined her work. The garden looked colorful and inviting, and she just knew the kids would be thrilled when they saw it. The past few months had been difficult for everyone, and while she could not give the twins Disney, she could give them a fun area of their own on the island.

She decided to take a quick break for lunch and to check on Ralphie, who happily played in his pen. She was relieved to find the grass intact and hoped that his digging phase would soon come to an end. Thunder rumbled in the distance, and she carried the puppy in with her as she went up to the attic to prepare lunch. The men were busy sanding, and she could see that the wallpaper in the living room was almost entirely gone. In the course of a few hours, Sam had done what would have taken her an entire week. Despite a few hiccups now and then with the crew, she was grateful for their presence.

Christina prepared turkey and cheese sandwiches with chips and brought them downstairs. By then, the storm had grown stronger, and the winds were blowing the trees so hard that many leaned and looked as if they might snap in half. Lightning flashed every few seconds, followed by thunder that shook the manor. Ralphie snuggled into the safety of her lap. She wrapped him in a blanket and held him tight to calm him while she and the men ate lunch and discussed renovations. They would apply the first stain downstairs later that day, so Christina would have to be careful to avoid walking on the floors unless absolutely necessary. She was happy to see that the men had been vacuuming wood dust as they sanded, so the mess was kept to a minimum. Sam would sand away the wallpaper in the cigar room next, and Christina thanked him once again for taking over the tedious task.

After lunch, the rain stopped, and Christina spent the afternoon working on the trail at the far side of the island, beyond the gardens and where it looked like it needed the most help. Dead branches had accumulated in several areas, especially with recent storms, making much of the pathway impassable. She gathered them into a wheelbarrow, emptying it every so often into what would become a large fire pit. She sprayed a weed killer on stray weeds that had cropped up and ran out after about a quarter of a mile. The men would have to bring more with them in the morning.

The air felt unseasonably chilly as she walked back to the manor, perfect for a cup of hot chocolate. She stopped to take a brief look at the product of her new-found green thumb. But as she drew closer, something about the garden seemed different. She stopped about ten feet from the mesh fence, quite sure her eyes were playing tricks on her. Or perhaps she was dehydrated…ill even. She sat down and took a few deep breaths, unsure of what was happening. It could not be. Yet when she looked again, she was horrified to see that her eyes were indeed truthful.

The peonies, that a few hours before were a swath of yellows, pinks, and reds, were now brown and dried out, as if they had died long ago and been left in the garden to wither. The tomato plants, many of which had tomatoes on them when planted, were black, as if they had been scorched. She picked up a tomato that had fallen to the ground, its color now a strange dichotomy of green on one side and black on the other and hardly distinguishable from the adjacent peppers and strawberries. It reminded Christina of looking at a black and white photo of something one knew well, such as a home or relative, fully expecting to see the color and vibrancy within the photo but seeing only a picture devoid of those traits that make it familiar.

Christina ran to the house. "Jason!" she called frantically from the front door.

Hearing her panic and fearing the intruder had returned, he ran out as quickly as he could, leaving the floor staining work behind.

"What's the matter?" He looked around, half expecting to find the man who had broken in.

"The garden." Christina pointed in the direction of the dead plants.

"Jeez," Jason responded when they got closer. The utter destruction was undeniable. "What happened? Did lightning strike it?"

"I…I don't know. It was perfect when I planted it," she said, trying to comprehend what had happened. She had planned this surprise for weeks, and now that she finally had time to do it, it was ruined. But saddest of all was the loss of a space the twins could call their own.

Sam and Jeremy joined a minute later, having picked up on the urgency in Christina's voice, and both were equally perplexed. Sam suggested that maybe there was something wrong with the soil, while Jeremy remained eerily quiet as he examined the destruction before him. Christina could sense that the scene made him uncomfortable, but did not pry. The group decided it best to remove the garden and worked in silence as they relocated plant remnants to the fire pit. The area quickly resumed its usual appearance, devoid of any evidence it had gone through the adventure of being a garden for the past few hours. Christina carried the posts and netting back to the basement storage room just in case she worked up the courage to try again. She felt a chill down her back as she quietly added the garden incident to the growing list of unsettling occurrences on the island and lingered on the basement steps for a moment to regain her composure before rejoining the men upstairs.

Dark, thunderous clouds loomed above, threatening the serenity of the peaceful evening. Sam and Jeremy hurriedly made their exit to the barge. Although it was a short distance to the mainland, they were well aware that turbulent weather could trap them on the island, and both were eager to return to their families for the weekend. Jason offered to make dinner that night and was cooking pasta when Christina went downstairs to grab some jarred sauce from the basement pantry.

The men had put down a coat of polyurethane on the second floor the day before, and the dark hardwoods shone like they were brand new. The hall window had been left open to air out the fumes, and a light breeze made its way through, catching Christina off guard and nearly making her drop the jar. Thunder rumbled in the distance, and she closed the window before continuing her ascent upstairs.

Suddenly, the hairs on the back of her neck stood up. Something, or someone, was there with her. She knew it. She could feel it. It was all around her. But glance down the stairwell and hallway revealed no one, and for a moment, she blamed the perpetual dimness of the lighting and silently chastised herself for neglecting to call an electrician. Just as she was about to dismiss the feeling entirely, the events of the day grew even more bizarre. The window that she had closed just seconds before, absent of window treatments for the duration of renovations, was now draped in heavy, red velvet curtains with gold cord edging. The grandiosity of style represented a fashion more akin to that popular a century or more ago. Stranger still, they resembled nothing she had seen stored away in the manor.

A polished, wooden accent table sat beside the window, supporting a green plant and kerosene lantern. A porcelain coffee cup and saucer, decorated in finely-painted flowers, sat along the edge, as if someone had set it down briefly and would be back in a moment to reclaim it. Christina's mind grappled with what her eyes saw but what could not possibly be. There had been no furniture in the hallway for days due to the floor refinishing. She stared at the table and curtains, unable to understand where they came from.

And just as she thought it could not get any stranger, it did. The hallway walls, bare from sanding, were covered in a golden wallpaper, its crest motifs shiny against a flat background and reflecting what little light was present. There were paintings, too, and a large, ornate mirror hung along the wall as if it had always been there.

The unfamiliar voices of a man and a woman echoed down the hallway. She heard the shuffle of a large hoop skirt as the woman, brunette hair pulled back and covered by a bonnet, and a gentleman wearing a gray tuxedo and top hat, walked down the hall twenty or so feet away, arguing in hushed tones about something indistinguishable. Neither seemed to notice her, and Christina stood in silence watching, too shocked to move. He grabbed the woman's arm, and she pulled her arm back forcefully, looking angrily at the gentleman, who proceeded to slap her face. She let out a horrendous scream and fled down the stairs. He stood watching her for a second before turning to go upstairs, seemingly unaware of Christina's presence as he walked past her. She followed slowly behind, careful to avoid the steps that squeaked, and watched as he entered the observatory on the third floor. He walked past the telescope and towards the windows, staring out, studying the stars that only he could see on this cloudy day. As Christina neared, she could see that he was, in fact, focused on the chapel, his hands writhing uncomfortably behind his back. He seemed to be in deep thought, and his face depicted an internal torment that she did not understand. He twisted the latch of a window and pushed it forward and, much to Christina's horror, climbed towards the ledge. She rushed towards him, begging for him to climb back in, but he took no notice, as if he could not hear her. And then he jumped, arms outstretched, as if expecting to fly, yet fell to the ground with an audible thump. She screamed and dropped the sauce she had been holding, chards of glass now surrounding her feet, and hardly seemed to notice the pain as she ran to the window, fully expecting to find a man lying seriously injured or dead on the ground below. But an equally horrifying sight met her frightened gaze. All appeared as it should. There was no mess of blood and guts that one might expect to find after a fall…in fact, there was no one to be seen anywhere. It was as though the gentleman with the top hat had just vanished…or perhaps never existed at all.

And then she saw it…the creature that wandered the halls at night and stalked Chelsea's dreams. It stood by the chapel, cloaked in darkness, watching. Its red, piercing eyes bore into her soul with an evil that transcended space and time. Its mouth transitioned into a snarl, baring fang-like teeth, as it let out a wicked laugh that echoed across the grassy field, creating reverberations that pierced the ears and shook the home, causing trinkets on a nearby table to rattle. It turned, its cloak swinging behind, and walked through the stone wall of the chapel. So that is where it hides, she thought.

Then, a woman's anguished wailing could be heard coming from one of the lower floors. Christina needed to know who this woman was. She sprinted in the direction of the noise, searching every bedroom and the entirety of the first floor. And as she passed room to room, she came to the quite frightening realization that the rest of the house, absent of furniture earlier in the day, was now immaculately furnished and decorated, matching the old-fashioned style of the upstairs hallway. Fine wallpaper adorned the walls. Clean linens covered the beds. A vase with a fresh bouquet of flowers sat in each room, as if ready to accept a new guest at a moment's notice. The manor was changing before her eyes back to what it had been in a prior lifetime.

The cries were everywhere, yet nowhere, and emanated from the walls, the floors, the ceiling. There was no escaping it. Terrified, she ran back upstairs, passing the hallway window, which once again stood open, the rain seeping into the house and onto the newly-finished floors. The curtains swayed in the heavy wind, which had blown several of the wall paintings, causing them to hang crookedly.

She did not stop to close the window a second time and instead, sprinted to the attic and into the arms of Jason, who was shocked to find her covered in tomato sauce and blood.

"What happened? Are you okay?" Jason set down his spatula and helped Christina over to a chair. "Did you step on glass?" he asked, more concerned, having noticed the bloody footprints along the floor. Before she could even answer, he had already pulled out several pieces, injuring his own hand in the process. Once each of the glass chards was removed, he washed and bandaged her feet.

In the pit of her stomach, she understood that what she had experienced was evil, and her primary impulse was to run and never return. Nervously, almost too afraid to talk, she asked if he had heard the crying or had felt the manor shake. Jason put down the bandage box he was holding and stood silently for a moment, listening, trying to hear what Christina was hearing, yet noticing nothing amiss. He reassured her that it was probably just the sound of an animal that she was hearing. She felt angry that he did not believe her but caught herself before saying something she would regret.

"Did you move furniture back downstairs?" Christina asked, knowing full well that he had not.

"No, why would I have done that? The floors aren't ready." Jason had a puzzled look on his face. He wondered where this was going.

"Come look." She pulled his arm behind her, still shaking, down the bloodied steps and to the second-floor landing. Yet, to her utter shock, the hallway stood empty, devoid of the accent table, plant, kerosene lantern, coffee cup, curtains, paintings, and mirror. Even the wallpaper had vanished, the walls returning to their freshly-sanded state. The window had closed, although the rain that had seeped inside remained the sole evidence of what had transpired.

Jason seemed confused. "Look at what?"

She grabbed his hand, pulling him to the bedrooms, which once more sat empty, and then to the first floor, eager to prove that she was not crazy. Yet it, too, had returned to its familiar state, absent of sofas, its walls bare, and plastic hanging from the ceiling to the floor just as it had before.

"Where are you going?" Jason called after her as she ran outside. She needed to know if someone was inside the chapel. She ran shoeless, feet bandaged, across the greenery and then breathlessly flung open the double, red-painted doors, fully expecting to confront the cloaked figure, perhaps surrounded by personal effects and other evidence of hiding out in the structure. But to her confusion, and also relief, there was no one and no trace of anyone having been there.

"Would you mind telling me what is going on?" Jason asked, running up behind her and seemingly just as perplexed as her.

"He was here! I saw him."

"Who was here?"

"The intruder!"

"You saw him?" Jason scanned the room, angry at the brazen attitude of the trespasser. He quickly canvassed the area, looking in and behind the church and along the tree line while Christina waited beside the chapel. By the time he returned, she was feeling rather poorly. Sweat beaded along her forehead, her eyes felt heavy, and her limbs could barely move from weakness.

Jason felt her flushed cheeks. "You're burning up. Let's get you back, away from this horrible place," he said, glancing at the chapel. Christina knew that he felt the evil within, too. He quickly closed the church doors and carried her, now too weak to walk, up to the attic. Her temperature reading came back at one hundred six degrees, and Jason started to worry he was going to have to bring her to the hospital. He could call Jeremy and have him bring the barge back to take her, but he did not want to do that unless he needed to because another thunderstorm was coming in just behind the last. The winds were picking up, which could make for a treacherous trip.

"Eat this popsicle," he ordered, handing her the dessert and an icepack to put on her face. He was very concerned about the fever and the obvious hallucinations Christina seemed to be experiencing. She had been weak and tired off and on now for weeks, and he began to fear that there was an illness of some sort that needed to be addressed. Perhaps she had scratched herself working outside and gotten an infection. Or maybe she had gotten a tick bite that they had not discovered while biking on the mainland.

Looking out the window, he could see large waves crashing against the shoreline. Lightning flashed brightly, illuminating the grounds below, and he knew that they had no choice but to wait out the storm. Christina sucked on the popsicle and fell asleep on the bed. Jason stayed by her side, periodically checking her fever and bringing fresh ice packs, until eventually, he fell asleep by her side.

By the following morning, the storm had given way to blue skies, but a heaviness remained, as if a dark cloud had engulfed the island. An inescapable feeling of impending doom took over, and Christina found it more and more difficult to find any areas of solace on the property. Everywhere she walked, she felt watched…stalked, really, a feeling she could only analogize to an animal being hunted by a predator.

She felt lucky to have Jason caring for her as she recovered, her fever now dissipating. He brought her ice cream, peanut butter crackers, and iced coffee, and she felt her strength slowly return. But the motivation to push forward with work had dropped. The night terrors and feverish visions and the mysterious intruder that seemed to come and go at will were almost too much to handle. For the first time, she found herself missing the predictability of her career and longing for the day that she opened her own practice.

It was so rare these days for someone to call her that she jumped when her phone rang. Her parents were deceased, and she and her sister, Eliza, had a strained relationship and only called each other on birthdays and holidays, if that. The caller ID showed John's number, and the realization that Charlie and Chelsea were due back the following day suddenly hit, as did the fact that she had neglected to call them at any point on their vacation. How could she have not remembered to check in? Had she really been so distracted that she had completely forgotten about the twins?

"John? Oh, hi!" she said, sounding caught off guard.

"Where have you been? I've been trying to get a hold of you for the past two days." He sounded more annoyed than worried.

"Two days? I guess I haven't had my phone on me. How are the kids? Are they having a good time?"

"They're having a blast. Chelsea got to eat breakfast with Cinderella, and Charlie…well, he has been more interested in reading than going on any rides." There was a long pause that followed, and Christina wondered whether she had lost the call.

"Are you still there?"

"Yeah, I'm here. Listen, is everything okay there?" he asked.

"Of course. Why wouldn't it be?"

He cleared his throat. "Chelsea tells me that you had someone break into the house. Why didn't you tell me?" The truth of it was that Christina did not want him to find out. She knew he would not want to kids to stay there any longer and, being unwilling to take them in himself, would insist she return to the mainland. "Do you think it's safe to have the kids there, I mean, if someone, obviously, knows how to get into the home?"

"We had a break-in," she admitted, yet she refrained from mentioning that the intruder had returned. "No one was hurt, and nothing was taken. I'm afraid to ask, but where is this going?" She began to grow angry. She knew full well what John had up his sleeve, and she did not like it.

"Chrissy." She had once loved his nickname for her but, since the divorce, had grown to resent it. "Chelsea has had nightmares about the intruder almost every night since we picked her up. We have barely slept this past week. She is terrified of that place."

"She's always had nightmares. It's just a phase, and she'll grow out of it."

"But she's never been like this. Screaming and kicking her legs, like she's fighting something in her sleep. Waking up in a cold sweat and shivering." Another pause followed. "Listen, I don't think she should go back. Or Charlie, for that matter. And I'm putting my foot down on this one. How long is it until you're finished with that place?"

"I mean, I don't know. A month…maybe two at the longest. John, I promised to get this done. I can't just pick up and leave. They love it here, too…both of them. Besides, we've had one of the workers staying with us since the break-in."

But she had to be honest with herself in that moment. How much good had been done by Jason living there? The intruder had still returned and obviously was not afraid of going into the home. What if he hurt one of the children? The simple logic of the situation had seemed lost on her the past few weeks, as if she had been in a fog and unable to clearly think about her kids' wellbeing, and that scared her more than anything. Up until the move, she had been hypervigilant about their safety and never would have allowed them to live under such circumstances.

"I'd like for them to stay with Rachel and me until you're done. We have room for them, and I realized this past week that I have not been spending the time with them they deserve. Maybe it would help you to be able to focus and get finished up more quickly, too."

Christina rolled her eyes at the statement. She wanted so badly to dismiss his concerns but could not, and despite his selfishness in the marriage and past indifference towards spending time with the twins, she had to applaud his efforts to include them in his life, however short-lived it may be.

"May I talk to them?" she asked, eager to hear their familiar voices.

She could hear John call for them. "Mom, we saw Mickey and got to go swimming, and I read four books!" Charlie exclaimed excitedly.

"And I got to ride all the rides. Charlie was too scared, though," Chelsea chimed in.

"Was not!" he yelled.

"It sounds like you had fun! I wish I could have been there too." A part of her envied Rachel for getting the opportunity to spend this time with them. She wondered if she would ever get the chance to take them to Disney World. "Hey guys, Mommy has an important question to ask you. Would you like to stay with your dad for a few weeks while I finish some important projects at the manor?"

"I want to stay with you," Charlie begged. He was much closer to Christina than John and missed playing with Ralphie and helping the crew with little tasks.

"I'll stay with Dad!" Chelsea exclaimed, excited to once again have her own room and be the center of attention. She thought Rachel was fun and enjoyed the crafts they did together. But more importantly, she was afraid of the manor and the cloaked man that lived in it. In fact, she dreaded the thought of returning. "Charlie, let's stay with Dad. Pleeeeaaase," she begged.

"Okay," he reluctantly agreed. As much as he wanted to return, he did not want to be there alone…without Chelsea, that is. Something scared him about the place, and it helped to have someone to confide in. "We can stay with Dad."

So, it was decided that the twins would stay with John. It pained Christina to let go…to let her ex-husband have control over the children's day-to-day lives when he seemed to have little interest before…but she reminded herself that sometimes people change when you least expect it. And as much as she hated to admit it, John was right about the safety risk. So, with a heavy heart, she told the children goodnight and that she loved them. She made sure they knew she would be finishing up work soon, and then their lives would go back to normal.

That night, Chelsea slept through the night, as peacefully as a baby snuggled in its mother's arms. She wrapped the blankets around herself tightly and pulled her teddy bear close to her chest, sleeping sans nightmares through to morning. It was as if a switch had been hit, and suddenly, the night terrors were a thing of the past.

But for Christina, nightmares were becoming a routine form of sleep interference, only adding to her growing fatigue. The dreams centered on the intruder. Sometimes, he watched her as she worked around the house, moving from room to room in silence, glaring at her with pure hatred. Other times, he pursued her around the property, her movements slowed as if running through jell-o, only to narrowly escape. She found herself wondering if there was a real connection between these nightmares and what she was experiencing at Statham Manor.

With the passage of time, there was an ever-growing sense of uneasiness in the waking hours as well. As she tidied the trail and cleared the gardens of debris, she caught herself looking over her shoulder, fully expecting someone to be watching from the shadows, only to see no one. Nightmares were becoming enmeshed with reality, and at times, she found it difficult to decipher whether she was awake or asleep. There was no safe place anymore. The omnipresent dark energy that infiltrated every corner seemed focused on Christina, and up until this point, Jason had not experienced more than a sighting of the intruder. She found herself left to carry the bulk of the burden herself and a growing resentment towards his blissful ignorance.

A few days of relative quietness passed. She had been working on a section of trail that had become crowded with weeds. It was a hot day, and on her way back to the manor for water, she stopped in front of the chapel, afraid of, but also morbidly curious about, it. The innocent-looking stone building, with its stained glass window of Jesus leading sheep through a pasture, exuded the false impression of holiness to the naïve. She oddly felt compelled to touch it, something she had thus far avoided, and as her hand contacted the cold stone, an evil radiated from the structure as fire radiates from a burning home. It felt like fear and anger and hate and sadness, all wrapped up into an energy thrown her way. Its flames jumped up her arm, then settled briefly back a few inches from her fingertips before jumping towards her heart, as if to capture her soul. She quickly pulled back her arm and turned, sprinting towards the manor and up the steps, past the three bewildered men who were in the final stages of finishing the first floor. She buried her head in her pillow and let out a scream, confident that no one would be able to hear her.

Jason opened the door a moment later. "Hey, I saw you run up here. Is everything okay?"

"There's something really wrong here…on the island, I mean." She wanted to tell him about the feeling of being watched and the evil that seemed to stalk her, but without any concrete evidence, felt stifled into silence.

"Did you see the intruder? Is he back?" He stood up, looking out the window, as if ready to break kneecaps if necessary.

"No, something else is going on. I don't know what…something I can't explain." She looked down. She was too afraid of possible judgment to talk about what really was happening. Would Jason think she was crazy? Would he leave her just as John had? The fear of him not believing her led her over and over again to keep it to herself.

"I think I might know what you mean." For a second, Christina was certain she had misheard. Then he pulled out a newspaper clipping from *The East Hampton Chronicles* that he had been carrying under his arm. "I found this repairing a floorboard that came loose. It sounds like the house has some history to it." The July 5, 1927 article entitled *Two Deaths on Private Island Belonging to Oil CEO Investigated as a Murder-Suicide* read…

Two bodies were discovered Saturday morning at Statham Manor. The estate sits on a private island just off the East Hampton coast and is home to the famed Elizabeth and George Statham of Statham Oil Productions. A landscaper for the socialites reportedly informed authorities after discovering the bodies of two maids. Their deaths have been preliminarily ruled a murder-suicide,

A black and white photo of Statham Manor stood next to the passage. It was easily recognizable by its stone structure, third-story windows, and round brick drive, although it lacked the greenhouse and boasted of impeccably maintained shrubbery and lawns.

"Wow, I had no idea something like that happened here. Did you?"

"I've heard rumors about the manor from older folks in town. I knew there were a few deaths here over the years, but never the specifics. Honestly, I thought much of it to be idle gossip, if you want me to be honest. Maybe this has something to do with the screaming you heard the other day. Maybe you're picking up on something that happened a long time ago."

There was a sense of relief knowing that Jason did not think she was crazy. "Annette never told me about any of this, but maybe she didn't know." But then again, Annette had not disclosed the manner in which her uncle passed away on the property either.

"I'll tell you what. How about you and I take the morning tomorrow to visit the local historical society and do a little digging into the home? Sam and Jeremy can remove the basement kitchen appliances pretty easily, so I don't think they'll mind me being gone for a few hours, especially since we're a little ahead of schedule."

Feeling recovered from her recent bout of sickness, Christina was eager to get off the island and would have jumped at the opportunity for just about any reason. She needed to know more about the place that was wreaking such havoc on her life and hopefully return with enough knowledge and willpower to finish renovations quickly. Jason's discovery acted as a reminder of how little she knew of the manor that increasingly seemed to be shrouded in mystery.

Chapter Seven

The East Hampton Historical Society did not open for another fifteen minutes. Christina and Jason walked past the white picket fence and a large wooden sign that read *Home Sweet Home Museum* and towards the front door of the two-story, cedar building. Neither had researched a home's history before, and the experience was an adventure of sorts for both of them.

They were surprised when the front door swung open, and an older woman answered. She had graying hair pulled back into a bun and wore an eighteenth-century dress over a hoop skirt and black boots that reminded Christina of a witch costume she once wore for Halloween. "Good morning," the woman exclaimed cheerfully, motioning for them to enter. "I'm Susan. Are you here for a tour? We usually do tours on Friday afternoons, but Martha here," she said, glancing behind her to another woman of similar age and attire, "would be happy to show you around the Town House and Clinton Academy. We also have several other homes and buildings within walking distance that we can tell you how to get to," she offered, smiling.

"Nice to meet you. I'm Christina," she introduced as the trio made their way inside. Martha had seemingly disappeared from the old wooden desk that sat beside the entryway, and Susan's eyes darted around the small giftshop, trying to find her. "We're not here for the tour," Christina explained.

"Well, what can I help you with, dear?"

"We are renovating Statham Manor and would like to get a little history on the place to help us restore it back to its original state. Are you familiar with the property?"

"Oh, of course. Everyone around here knows about it. It was once a pillar of this community, full of fancy parties hosting the rich and famous. But it seems to have been forgotten these last few decades. Such a shame. You said you're fixing it up?"

"Yes, and we would like to know as much about the property as possible," Christina responded.

"Come with me," she said and began the walk across the museum, past the gift shop and shelves of artifacts set out neatly on display, finally stopping at what looked like a storage room, filled with boxes from floor to ceiling. The boxes contained historical documents for older homes and buildings in the area, but despite the cluttered appearance, she assured Christina that it was an organized mess. She proudly described how she had labeled and alphabetized each box personally when hired nearly twenty years prior. "You would not believe what a disaster it was before I came," she laughed. Very quickly, she was able to find two boxes bearing the name Statham Manor.

"Help yourself. We just ask that you sit at one of the tables." She pointed to the library-style tables in the middle of the room, dimly lit by table lamps. "We try to avoid having older papers exposed to direct sunlight. We also have gloves on each table that we prefer you wear while handling the documents. And if you take any photos, please make sure that the flash is off. Let me know if you need any assistance," she said cheerfully as she began to exit the room.

"Oh, please stay…if you can, of course. We would love to ask some questions as we go through the materials."

Christina noticed a peculiar look on Susan's face as she glanced around the room a bit nervously, and she wondered if there was something that made her uncomfortable about Statham Island.

But if so, she said nothing of it and agreed to join them to review the documents.

The trio carried the documents over to the table. Between the two boxes were hundreds of documents. They wondered how a manor could harbor so much history and realized it was going to take much longer than just a morning to go through the paperwork.

Copies of the deeds to the island dated back to 1877, when the land was purchased by a Mr. George Statham. Susan told them that up until the early nineteenth century, it is believed that the island was inhabited by a tribe of Native Americans, although very little is known about them. A few relics, including clay pottery, arrowheads, and jewelry, were found as Statham Manor was being built and were currently displayed on the upstairs floor of the museum, having been donated by the original family years before. Susan asked if they would like to see the relics, but given how long it was going to take to review all of the documents, they politely declined.

A copy of a marriage certificate revealed that Mr. Statham had married Elizabeth Murray in 1875. He was thirty-five at the time, and she was nineteen. She was the daughter of a wealthy business owner in New York City, and there were rumors at the time of their nuptials that the marriage was a quid pro quo arrangement of sorts between her father and Mr. Statham. As the CEO of the hugely successful oil company Statham Oil Productions, Mr. Statham also had quite a bit of clout in the political environment of New York. When Mr. Murray's real estate company sold desirable, oil-laden land with pre-secured drilling rights to Statham Oil Productions followed by the marriage just months later, the new Mr. and Mrs. Statham quickly became the talk of the town and the victims of idle gossip.

It is believed that this was a deciding factor in Mr. Statham's selection of an island as their marital home. Mrs. Statham, as an attractive and wealthy young woman on her own accord, was hit particularly hard by the gossip. She found herself the butt of jokes, often made by other women harboring some level of jealousy towards her. But there was also a fascination with the couple. The marriage of a wealthy oil tycoon to a real estate socialite made them instant celebrities, and the intense interest in the couple led to invasions of privacy as paparazzi sought to capture images, particularly those that shed the couple in a poor light because of the larger price tag associated with such photos.

In one newspaper clipping, there was an article entitled *The Rise and Fall of the Stathams*. A black-and-white photo of the couple smiling on their wedding day stood juxtaposed with a later photo of the couple walking through New York City, the woman appearing to be in tears and evidently unaware that she was being photographed. The article talked about how the two were living in separate homes and that Mr. Statham had even taken on a mistress. It was a tabloid article of the olden days that had found its way to front-page headlines.

But in reality, the second photo told a very different story. The day it was taken, Mrs. Statham had gone to see a midwife in the city, excited to be pregnant with their first child, but had learned that the child had passed. Emotionally distraught, she cried as she made her way home, accompanied by Mr. Statham, unaware that anyone was watching. But someone at the paper happened to notice her holding her stomach as she left the midwife's home and then wrote a second article entitled, *Inside the Nursery of Socialite Elizabeth Statham*. And, of course, there was no nursery and no baby. When the Statham's caught wind of the articles, Elizabeth had a nervous breakdown that required institutional care for several weeks.

"At that point, Mr. Statham decided that enough was enough, and it was almost as if the two went into hiding," Susan continued.

They did not want the constant barrage of attention or candid photographs or any more of the gossip. They simply wanted to heal, away from the scrutiny of the public eye. And that is why an island as a place of residence was chosen. And this particular one happened to be close enough to civilization but far away enough for complete privacy."

In 1880, the manor was built. The island happened to be very rocky and provided an ocean of stones that were used to build the house. And because importing building materials was much more difficult at that time, using the native stone allowed for easier and quicker construction. Timber from the island was used for the structure. Glass and roofing were imported, and it is believed that much of the shrubbery and flowers were originally imported from England with the aid of an English landscaper.

The Statham's eventually had four children, two boys and two girls. And once the children arrived, the couple began to resume their socialite identity. Lavish parties were held on the island, and it was quite the talk of locals when ferries were seen carrying other famed personalities back and forth across the water. Those in East Hampton speculated as to what went on at the parties. Some thought that there were large orgies. Others thought that there was a cult of sorts, an elite club that only the wealthiest and most successful were invited to join. This club would allow CEOs to form under-the-table deals that, if true, violated conflict of interest and ethical guidelines in the business world.

Susan continued, "There was a concerted effort to out the family with the use of spies. One spy in particular, Nina, was hired by a competing oil company to listen in on conversations, especially between Mr. Statham and the gentlemen guests, and relay information back about anything possibly incriminating. She worked as a nanny for the family and found it easy enough to sit in the hidden staircases after putting the children to bed, listening to conversations on the other side of the wall. When the gentlemen moved to the cigar room, she would sneak back to her quarters in the basement, which happened to sit directly below the cigar room and had very little noise insulation, and listen more. She took notes in a journal, which she hid under her mattress, and on her monthly day off, would bring the evidence to her boss for review. For each journal she provided, she was paid a hefty two hundred dollars. It was a good side hustle that was helping her save up so that one day, she could be free to do as she pleased, provided she was able to continue to escape marriage by dressing in a homely fashion." Susan chuckled.

"But one day, she stopped traveling to see the businessman, and he never heard from her again. And with no family living and no husband, her lack of sightings did not set off any alarms. Eventually, the Statham's placed an ad in the local paper for a "nanny to four loving children." No one dared disrespect the Statham's by asking why the old nanny left, as it would imply that they thought that she possibly was not happy in her position. So the question remained…where was Nina Mable? It was a question that, to this day, had never been answered. Some speculated that she finally had married and moved away, but local conspiracy theorists thought that she had been killed by a member of the Statham's inner circle and her body buried on the property. Of course, there was no evidence to support any of that."

"That's quite the story," Christina replied. She had pulled out a newspaper article and placed it in front of Susan. "Was the manor used as an orphanage?" she asked, hoping the answer was no, but knowing from the article that it had been, and felt a deep sense of sadness at the news.

The 1943 article entitled *Three-Year-Old Orphan Boy Drowns at Statham Manor* revealed…

The body of three-year-old Alexander Miller was found Wednesday morning by a boater traveling just south of Statham Island. He was identified as the boy who went missing after playing unsupervised by the water with his five-year-old sister, who told investigators that another little boy, whose identity remains unknown, beckoned Alexander towards the water. A second boy has yet to be found. Mrs. Donaldson, the orphan keeper, has confirmed that the remaining ten children are safe and denied that any other children had been on the shore that day.

Most Holy Trinity Parish, a Catholic parish in East Hampton, has offered to hold a mass and bury the child at the orphanage. Funeral arrangements are pending.

"Yes, it was used as an orphanage during the 1940s after the last surviving Statham child, Sylvia, sold the property in the late 1930s. It is believed that by that point, the Statham inheritance had largely run dry, and the cost of maintaining the island was simply too much. So, it was sold to a couple who opened an orphanage. Many men from the area had died in the war, and often, in those days, mothers would die in childbirth or from illness, and the children were left with no one. It was a difficult time, especially for the children of our community."

"Was the other child ever found?"

"Sadly, he wasn't. No one ever found out who he was."

"That's horrible." The story reminded her that she needed to keep a closer eye on Charlie and Chelsea should they return to the island. They were still learning to swim, and the danger of being surrounded by water felt more real than ever, knowing that a drowning had already happened on the property.

The orphanage documents appeared to be organized in a pile together. Jason handed over another document, hoping Susan could shed light on this next one. The article was darker and talked of allegations of abuse by the orphan keepers.

"I don't like to talk about this," she warned. "A gentleman who provided groceries and other necessities to the island was met by a young child during one of his deliveries. He noted the child appeared malnourished and filthy. It was a child he had known from prior visits to be healthy and robust. After reporting the incident to the Children's Bureau, an investigation was initiated into the operation of the orphanage. A report of extreme neglect was created after it was discovered that the children living at the orphanage had not received more than one meal per day for the past two months. An older orphan girl, aged ten, was found caring for the other children as best she could while the orphan keepers, a man and a woman, were found barricaded in the attic. They talked of hearing voices and believed someone, or something, was out to get them. Both were institutionalized for schizophrenia, and the orphanage was subsequently closed."

"How incredibly sad." Christina could hardly believe what she was hearing. So much tragedy in one place. And those poor children. It made her shiver to think that she had so nonchalantly allowed her children to stay at a place with such a history. If she had known, she would have thought twice about taking the job at Statham Manor.

"It's been a black eye on the community for nearly eighty years now. No one likes to talk about what happened there all those years ago. Many in town look forward to the revamping of the island and are hoping its tragic history can be…made up for, if you will."

She set aside the last article into the pile forming beside her and glanced down at her watch, announcing that it was already eleven fifteen and that she needed to take her lunch break. "Diabetes, you know. It gets the best of us. I'll send in Martha in case you have more questions," she said, excusing herself.

A few quiet minutes passed with Christina and Jason discussing what they had just heard. Despite having lived and worked in the area for nearly two decades, Jason was surprised by how much he had not known about the island. It seemed to him that many in town had kept the unflattering pieces tucked under the rug, perhaps to avoid tainting the town's image.

Martha's attire so closely matched Susan's that Christina wondered whether there was a uniform or dress code that they had to adhere to or whether they chose to dress alike. She had slightly less graying than Susan and dark brown eyes, their softness hidden behind bifocal lenses. Without those differences, one could be easily confused with the other.

"Ah, I see you've found the piece on Ronald Whittaker," she said, pointing at the newspaper clipping Jason had been reading over while they waited. A picture of candles and a pentagram stood at the top, followed by an opinion piece by a Mr. Peter Willis of *The East Hampton Daily* discussing whether unsavory, pagan practices should be tolerated within the community. In it, he alleges that Mr. Whittaker, who purchased the property in the early 1960s, regularly held séances at the home, during which he and guests would sit within a chalk-drawn pentagram, ironically drawn on the chapel floor, and with the aid of a spirit board, attempt to contact those who passed away on the property. The group apparently believed that Elizabeth and George Statham had had business competitors, and even their own nanny, killed and had buried them on the property. They sought to discover answers in regard to the alleged murders. Mr. Willis ended his article with a warning: *If our community continues to tolerate the evil practice of contacting the dead, how*

"Yes, we love the infamous around here," she joked. "People were more superstitious back then, and as you can imagine, Mr. Whittaker's alleged séances made him an outcast in town. The rumor that people were buried on the property was never taken seriously. This article actually sparked a lawsuit between him and *The East Hampton Daily*. He believed that the knowledge of his séances scared away potential business patrons at the restaurants he owned around town and ultimately hurt him financially."

"What was the outcome?" Christina asked, intrigued but already knowing that Mr. Whittaker most likely won the defamation lawsuit. Although she worked in the area of medical malpractice, she had discussed many similar cases with colleagues at the firm, enough to know that a judge and jury would have likely sided with the gentleman whose livelihood was destroyed based upon unsubstantiated claims with the purpose of creating a sensational headline.

"Oh, Mr. Whittaker walked away with thirty thousand dollars, I believe. It was a substantial sum in those times, enough to warrant leaving his flailing businesses behind to start over somewhere else. After he left, no one wanted anything to do with the island. Many locals thought it was cursed, and it sat vacant until a couple from out of town bought it in the '80s…Nellie and Lorenzo Malone. They had high hopes of turning the island into some sort of tourist destination. They were middle-aged and hired a contracting crew to help renovate, and they managed to get quite a bit done. But that first winter in the home was usually cold, with snow accumulating two feet at times. They were left to do much of the renovating themselves because the crews simply could not reach the island. Within a few months of moving in, both came down with pneumonia and died within one week of each other. It was so sad…another tragedy for the town and for me," she said regretfully.

"How did you know them?" Christina asked, hoping she was not being too nosy.

"They were my parents."

"I'm so sorry," she quickly replied. She had not meant to trigger an unpleasant and personal memory.

"Oh, it was a long time ago now. I had been away at college when I got the call. I didn't even know they had been sick, so you can imagine the guilt I felt for not having been there to help them. Luckily, I had a lot of family who helped me get through that part of my life. I found out later from an aunt that my mother had been seeing ghosts and became ill following a particular scary encounter."

"I'm sure that was very difficult for you," Christina replied. But her mind wandered frantically as she thought about the afflictions and deaths affecting nearly all inhabitants of the island. There certainly seemed to be a dark trend. The frightening revelation was not lost on Jason, who, as of late, had been experiencing sudden motivation to close up shop on the island, even if it meant he and the crew would have to cut some corners to finish more quickly. Each document uncovered made him worry more for the safety of Christina and himself at the manor, and he began to wonder whether there was something more to the sudden departure of Albert, the long-standing employee who had worked with him and Jeremy for years before suddenly and inexplicably leaving everything behind…his work, his home, his friends. The *why* had been on his mind ever since. Perhaps he had been driven away by something Jason did not understand…and for the first time, he entertained the idea that perhaps something paranormal was at play. He shivered, and his hair stood on end as he thought about how many deaths had occurred on the property and had to remind himself that tragedy is just an unfortunate part of life that must be accepted and expected, as his father had liked to say.

The two learned that after the deaths of the Malones, the island sat abandoned for fifteen years before being purchased at a steep discount at auction by a Mr. Robert Jameson in 2015. He had intended to turn the island into a bed and breakfast escape that offered canoeing, a butterfly garden, biking trails, beach access, gold searches, and even ghost walks. But as Christina was now acutely aware, he died suddenly and unexpectedly in a manner that haunted her more than any ghost possibly could.

It was the early afternoon, and Christina and Jason needed to get back to the island if they were to get anything done that day. They thanked Martha for her time. She was sad to see them go, as there was much more she hoped to tell them about the property, and they had only gotten through one box of paperwork.

"Come back if you want to go through any more of the documents or if you have questions. Obviously, Statham Island does not have the best reputation, but don't let that worry you too much. A few tragedies shouldn't ruin a beautiful place forever, should they?" She sounded as if she was trying to convince herself, though, and Christina and Jason nodded in feigned agreement. Walking out, they gave a friendly wave and thank you to Susan, who had returned to the main lobby of the museum from lunch.

"Did you find what you were looking for?" she asked, helpfully.

"Yes, thank you, and Martha was very helpful."

After they had left, Martha and Susan sat together in the lobby. No other visitors had come that day, so it was just the two of them. The cousins had always worked together and dressed alike and, in their older years, had started to look almost like sisters.

"Do you think that creature is still there?" Susan asked in a hushed tone, despite the absence of others besides themselves.

"I don't know. But I could tell she knew something was going on. Why else would she be so interested in the history of a place she's just renovating? People who are just there to do a job normally wouldn't want to waste time researching the place."

"Poor woman. A little strange, but I feel sorry for her. I hope she got what she needed and, for God's sake, leaves that evil place."

"Shhh," Martha said, putting her finger over her mouth, as if worried the walls might overhear. "How much longer do you think she'll last?"

"I'd give her a few days. If she's seen it, as I suspect, it won't be long now. I just hope she gets out before it's too late."

Christina and Jason stopped at the local post office where the mail belonging to the Statham residence had piled up after several weeks of neglect. She could not possibly haul the armful back with her and, stepping away from the high-traffic areas, sorted through what warranted opening versus what could be discarded before they left.

Most of the mail had been sent out indiscriminately and consisted of maid and lawn care services and advertisements for local businesses. There was a local newspaper with the town's most recent news, business listings, and future events.

And then there was a postcard from Disney World that had been stamped two weeks prior, addressed to Christina. The front had a picture of Cinderella's castle with the words, 'Greetings from a Magical World!' And on the back, Charlie, in his best writing, had written, 'Mommy, we mis you and wish you were her!' Chelsea had drawn a picture of a rainbow and a heart. She was not a confident writer yet and preferred drawing pictures. A tear rolled down her cheek as she read it. The gravity of not having them with her was starting to weigh heavily on her heart. Jason put his arm around her.

"You know; you don't have to do this. We've got the rest and can finish up."

"I promised Annette I'd do this. And we're almost done." She was not the type to give up and knew that it would only be a few more weeks until she was finished and life would regain some semblance of normalcy. But she still hated herself for it…for selfishly choosing a project over her babies, the very sort of thing she promised herself she would never do as a mother and one of the primary reasons she had chosen to move with them to the island in the first place.

A few more weeks, she told herself again as they boarded the barge. She placed the postcard into her purse, finding it difficult to look at. It made her question whether she was the good mother she thought she was.

While the town of East Hampton had been blanketed in sunshine, the island seemed dark and dreary, as if a storm cloud perpetually hung above. The manor was no exception, and the lack of adequate lighting made working in the evening nearly impossible, slowing progress. A nauseating feeling overcame Christina at the thought of having to spend another night there, knowing its history.

Sam and Jeremy had stripped the basement kitchen of all appliances and were busy hauling items to the barge. She was surprised to find that they had also gathered up the broken glass of the greenhouse into large, black garbage bags, and three piles of new window panes sat beside the structure, waiting to be placed. With the trail finally in order, replacing the windows was her next task.

"Did you bring glazing putty?" she asked Jeremy, knowing she would need it to set the new window panes into their frames.

"I knew we forgot something. We'll bring putty with us in the morning. Oh, Mike stopped by with more groceries while you were gone, so we brought them up to your suite. I hope that's okay."

Christina thanked him and walked inside. As renovation manager, she needed to periodically check their work and report back to Annette. She walked to the basement kitchen and was impressed by how much they had accomplished. Not only had the appliances all been removed, but the cabinets, too. Except for the pipes and wiring, one could not even tell that the space had ever been a kitchen.

She gave Annette a call to update her on the progress, and after Sam and Jeremy had left, she made some coffee for herself and Jason. But as she sat in the attic living room, waiting for the coffee to brew, she could not shake the feeling of being watched.

"Jason?" she asked, hoping that she was sensing him being nearby. But there was no answer. "Where are you?" Still no answer.

She went back to getting out coffee cups and filling them with coffee cream. Then, a cracking sound rang out so loudly it could not be ignored. She turned, startled, but could see nothing out of the ordinary.

"Jason?" she called again, louder this time.

"I'm down here," he called from the foyer.

Christina stood in silence, listening for anything else. There was only silence, except for the pounding of her heart, yet something was there. She slowed her breathing, afraid of what might appear at any minute, and then sprinted down both flights of stairs and into the safety of Jason's arms.

Chapter Eight

It had been several days since Ralphie had returned to the island. Jeremy's kids seemed intent on keeping the puppy with them, and without the twins to protest, there really was no reason to bring him along. Christina suddenly felt as though a punch had been launched at her belly. The absence of Ralphie served as a reminder that Charlie and Chelsea were not coming back. At times, the silence was so deafening and utterly depressing that she found herself unable to move, wanting nothing more than to abandon her work and return home. Yet, at other times, she felt strangely compelled to stay, a sense of dread overtaking her at the thought of leaving the grand manor behind to become nothing more than a tabbed entry in her memory bank.

Jeremy and Sam arrived early that morning and immediately got to work installing new kitchen cabinets and appliances. She welcomed the hammering and drilling, anything that brought life into the manor. Grabbing an old radio, she had found in the basement, she walked outside, happy to find the glazing putty she had asked for beside what remained of the greenhouse. She busily spent the next few hours scraping away the remaining glass from the frames and puttying in the new windows while listening to classic rock. Everything was peaceful, almost normal even.

Then, off in the distance, there was a sound that reminded her of her children's voices. She ignored it, knowing too well how the mind could play tricks, especially on an island such as this. She got back to work, puttying in another window, and then heard it again, only this time louder.

"Mom!" A voice came from the wood line, and Christina turned, stunned to see John, his hair freshly cut, walking up with the twins in tow. For a moment, the island's harshness softened. Even the clouds seemed to lift, and a sense of excitement overtook her as she rushed to hug them. They looked bigger than she remembered.

"What are you doing here?"

She hugged Charlie and Chelsea so tightly that Charlie yelled, "Ow!"

"Oh, I'm sorry, honey." She pulled the kids in for another hug, this one gentler than the last. It felt as though she had been struck by a beam of warm sunshine on a bitterly cold day.

"We decided to come up for a little visit. They wanted to surprise you, but I'll take them back with me later. I hope we're not interrupting." He looked tired, as if the long journey had been more than he had anticipated with two youngsters.

"No, of course not." Christina set down the putty. "So how did you all get out here?" she asked curiously, peeking around John towards the dock. She could see Mike's ferry puttering away from the shore and wondered whether he had been in on the surprise.

"Oh, it's not that hard to find a ferry," he laughed. Christina caught herself smiling.

The kids had run off towards the house. They missed their old room, and many of their toys remained upstairs. Charlie had left a few books that he wanted to bring back with him, and Chelsea remembered that her favorite teddy was still in her bed.

"Well, I wasn't expecting you. I mean, I'm glad you all came to see me, but I thought we agreed that they would stay off of the island. Perhaps it's not the best idea for you to be here."

"The kids have been asking for you nonstop. They wanted to surprise you, and we went through a lot of effort to get here. Don't you want to see them?" He had a puzzled look on his face, unable to comprehend her sudden standoffishness.

"Of course, but I thought…" she started, but hoping to avoid an argument, let it go. "Never mind. Come in. I'll make some lunch. The workers are busy in the main kitchen, so we'll have to go upstairs to the attic suite where I've been staying." Christina peaked into the basement, wanting to catch Jason and warn him of John's arrival, but he was nowhere to be found. As they walked up the stairs and into the suite, she wondered how John would react to seeing Jason's belongings. She had not told him that they were staying together and was not sure how he would feel about seeing another man's clothes strewn about the floor. But then she reminded herself of his own actions *within* the marriage and told herself that he could just deal with it. To her surprise, not a peep, not a single disapproving look, came from John as they walked through the attic. It was as though they had never been husband and wife at all. She doubted that she could have maintained such composure had she walked through Rachel's room.

The children were already in their room playing tic tac toe on scrap paper. She had missed the sound of their chatter and laughter and left the door to the kitchen open so that she could hear them while she prepared turkey sandwiches. John handed her condiments from the fridge as she worked, and for a moment, it felt like the old days.

"It's a beautiful house. Maybe I can get the grand tour later."

"Sure, if you want. The crew's been great. Everything looks much better than when we started. You wouldn't believe how rundown it was."

"How much longer do you expect renovations to take?" he asked bluntly.

"A few weeks, maybe a little longer, just depending on how quickly some odds and ends can be finished."

John was silent for a moment, and Christina knew that her answer was not what he was hoping for. She could see the dismay in his eyes and knew that he was not going to drop it. Here we go, she thought to herself.

"I don't think a few more weeks…or longer, God forbid…is going to work. Charlie and Chelsea need you and haven't seen you for weeks now. You don't even bother to call. Rachel and I are doing it all on our own. Can't you just leave this behind, just tell Annette that you've done your best and need to get back to the kids?"

Christina stopped, suddenly aware of what was going on. "You're tired of them, aren't you?" she shot accusingly. "Or is it Rachel? Does she want them out before the baby arrives? They're in your way, aren't they?" The words even surprised her, and the look on John's face indicated that he was just as shocked that the truth flowed with such accuracy from her lips.

"Of course I want them," he said defensively, trying to remain calm since the children were just one room over. "And Rachel does, too. But they *need* you!"

"I told you, I can't. I'm not going to break my promise to Annette. You and Rachel can find a way to make it work." Her cheeks flushed with anger. "Maybe if you had focused on your family instead of traveling the world with your mistress, we wouldn't be in this situation," she added, twisting the knife just enough to anger John. He slammed his fist on the counter, creating a resounding bang. He had never hit Christina but felt the sudden urge to slug her.

"I'm not the one who abandoned our kids to vacation on some island," he shot back.

Christina looked down. The words hurt more than she imagined they could. She would never abandon her children, and the decision to keep them off the island had been his own. The fact that John dared say something so hurtful only infuriated her more.

"Well, at least I didn't knock up some flying cocktail waitress. What is she, like twenty? How embarrassing." She was yelling, and the kids were listening to every word. She burst into tears when she saw them peek their heads around the kitchen door, trying to figure out what was happening. Never in her marriage had she and John fought with such hatred for each other.

"You know what? This was a mistake. Charlie, Chelsea, grab whatever you want to take with you. We're leaving." He got on his phone and made a call to The Stargaze Express, requesting that the ferry company return to the island to pick them up. He descended the stairs, brushing past Jason on his way down. John stopped briefly to look at him, but the men said nothing to each other and walked in their respective directions.

"Who was that?" Jason asked, pointing towards the stairs. Christina explained the surprise visit and that they had had an argument. It bothered her deeply that they had gone from cordiality just minutes before to being at each other's throats.

"Hi, guys!" Jason greeted the twins.

"Hi, Jason!" They yelled back in unison. They were excited to see him. Chelsea and Charlie both noticed that something about Jason seemed different. Chelsea thought that his hair looked lighter. Charlie thought he looked cold and needed a sweater. But neither dwelled too much on it.

"Christina, have you seen my watch? I left it on the nightstand, but it wasn't there when I got up this morning."

"I haven't, but I'll keep an eye out. Charlie, Chelsea, take these with you." She handed them their sandwiches. "And give this one to your dad. We had a little disagreement. We shouldn't have been so loud or said words like that."

"Are you mad at us, too?" Chelsea asked, tears welling up in her eyes. "We tried to be good."

"Of course not, sweetie. Sometimes, parents have fights, and it has nothing to do with you. I'm sorry you had to hear us."

"We were going to have a picnic, but now it's ruined." Charlie hung his head. Christina attempted to give him a hug, but he moved away.

"Do you two like staying with your dad and Rachel?" she asked, hoping to change the subject.

"It's fine," Charlie replied shortly. "But I liked it better when it was Dad and you."

"Remember what Dad said. They got a de-vor," Chelsea said, taking care to clearly state the last word. "Now we have two moms."

Christina could hear the ferry out on the water and, looking out the window, could see it docking.

"Come on, guys, it's time for you two to get back home. Mommy will be done here soon, and then we'll get back to normal. I promise," she said, squeezing them in close. She tried to be strong as she led them back to the dock and cried in silence as she waved goodbye, watching the ferry pull away with her most prized possessions aboard. What was she doing? She wanted so badly to leave with them that day, but something on the island was holding her back. Despite her growing hatred of the place, she could not leave even if she wanted to, just as an addict cannot give up their drug. And with a feeling of hopelessness, she walked in silence back towards the manor. The rain began to fall in heavy sheets, drenching her by the time she reached the front door.

"Rach, I'm telling you something is just not right up there. Chrissy..." Rachel gave him a look. She could not stand it when John referred to Christina by her old nickname, and despite his best efforts to avoid the triggering name, he continued to use it. He silently berated himself for doing it yet again. "I mean Christina...the kids' mom...what do you want me to call her?" It had become a point of contention between the two. "Something's very wrong over there. She was angry and argumentative, almost combative." He did not share that he, too, had felt irrationally angry while on the island and had a strong desire to hurt Christina, and it scared him. "She is not the same person. She looked sickly and frail, and her eyes almost had...oh, I don't know how to explain it...a darkness to them." He had thought about her eyes almost nonstop since his visit earlier that afternoon and how the lovely green shade had appeared almost black. Her hair, once a beautiful blonde, had become heavily streaked with gray. Her cheeks had sunken as an aging woman's would, revealing the sharpness of her cheekbones.

Rachel slipped her nightgown over her growing belly and joined John, who was sitting on the edge of the bed. She rubbed his shoulders. "Well, it sounds like we've done the right thing by keeping the kids here with us, then."

"I'm telling you, something is not right in that place. The kids are not going back." He hesitated to continue, afraid of what Rachel might think of his sanity. He decided it best to keep the rest to himself. He had learned over the years that discussions of the paranormal were not readily accepted by most, and he had a reputation to maintain, even if it was with Rachel. How could he describe what he saw without sounding crazy himself? "I'm going to reach out to Adam," he said, referring to his attorney, "and find out if there's a mental health examination of some sort that can be done to ensure she's mentally capable of caring for the children once this project of hers is finished. I don't want them going back to a nutcase."

It was not often that John talked negatively about his ex-spouse. It gave Rachel pleasure, in a sick sort of way, whenever he was at odds with Christina because it made her feel more confident that he would never go back to her. It was an unsubstantiated fear she had held since they began their relationship that periodically reared its ugly head. She needed to know that she was the only one he would ever consider spending his life with. She clutched her belly, reminding herself that, at least for now, the baby would keep him by her side.

Christina sat at the table in the newly refinished dining room. The room had been freshly wallpapered in an intricate gold and hunter green design. The art gallery had been re-hung, all of the paintings in their original order. And the golden, circa 1970, linen curtains had been replaced by green velvet curtains, flanked to either side of the window with golden cords, in keeping with the original style of the manor. The room looked ready to host a fancy party.

The heavy afternoon rains prohibited her from finishing the greenhouse. It would have to wait until the following day. Sam and Jeremy had left early after Jeremy's son had broken his arm on the monkey bars at school and would not return until after the weekend.

She began calling apartments in the Manhattan area to check for availabilities. It was time to plan for life after Statham Manor, and as a single mom, as the renovations were quickly winding down. But every call was a disappointment. Chelsea and Charlie were at the age that they needed their own rooms, and there were no three-bedroom apartments available for the next six months. She kicked herself for having waited so long to search, having forgotten how grueling the process could be in the city, and was reaching the conclusion that a search in the surrounding suburbs might be the only viable solution.

Her train of thought was suddenly broken by the horrible feeling that she had come to dread…the unmistakable sense of being watched. She sat still, only moving her eyes, as if sensing the approach of a predator. The room was perfectly silent, yet someone, or something, was indeed there. She had felt the evilness of it before. There was an overwhelming urge to run, but what from? Then, glancing up, was a reality equally, if not more, disturbing. The painting of the little boy playing with the kittens looked different, still recognizable, yet something had changed. She walked closer, slowly, eyes focused on what had been one of her favorite pieces in the manor, horrified to notice an evilness about the artwork. The boy's smile, once pleasant and sweet, extended upwards and outwards into a wicked grimace. The kittens, formerly full of life, were limp with lifelessness, the one held by the boy with its neck broken. The milk bowl sat filled with a dark, red substance that spilled in thick streaks over the bowl and onto the ground below.

Another heap of blood bubbled over the rim, this time dripping out of the picture and to the dining room floor, creating a crimson pool around her feet. Christina screamed, jumping back from the red puddle, blaming the sick hallucination on fatigue. She blinked, expecting to see the little boy in his normal state, holding and playing with kittens beside a bowl full of milk. But what stood before her had not changed for the better. No, now the little boy's eyes, which before had looked down upon the kittens lovingly, stared directly at her in an empty darkness. The boy's skin had taken on a scaly, alligator-like appearance that reminded her of the creature. She screamed louder and sprinted towards the foyer, turning back as she rounded the stairs. The eyes of the boy had followed, as if tracking her every move.

"Jason!" she yelled, but no one came. "Jason!" she yelled louder, more urgently, but still no response. Her gaze became fixed on the wall of oil paintings. The antique, beautifully painted portraits, which once brought her happiness, now offered only horror. Every man, woman, and child stared straight back, their eyes trained on her. A husband and wife painted on their wedding day stood dressed in a suit and black dress, their eyes beaded and dark, the bouquet withered and brown. An elderly man, whose gentle face reminded her of her own father's, now snarled, like an angry wolf ready to attack. For a second, she thought she saw a picture of herself with Jason, the two holding hands and smiling. But as she moved forward to look more closely, there was movement from a painting to the right, as a large, hairy spider emerged from the ear of a young man standing beside his greyhound, falling to the floor with an audible plop that could not be brushed off as a product of the imagination. Then, another plop as a large spider fell from the eye of an unsuspecting gentleman posing in a blue suit. Plop, plop, plop…the spiders continued to exit the orifices of those who dared be part of the gallery until the floor, covered in arachnids, took on a hellish resemblance of maggots, trampling each other in their quest to reach Christina. She stood frozen in time, too stunned to scream or move, even as the spiders reached her shoes and crawled up her ankles. It was as though she was an observer, watching her own destruction but unable to react. She was a prisoner, trapped into inaction by her own fear. In every painting, she saw the creature that roamed the manor. It was here.

She felt herself falling and, with a bang, hit the floor, losing consciousness in the process and slipping into a dream-like state. A man stood next to her, and she noticed he was holding her hand. He gave her a smile, and in her mind, as if he was guiding her, she could see his time on the island. He showed her images of renovating, and she felt his joy as he worked on the bed and breakfast he so desperately longed to open. Reluctantly, he shared images of himself drinking heavily as his mental state deteriorated, culminating in his suicide in the chapel. At that point, Bob forcefully grabbed Christina by the shoulders and, looking deep into her eyes, as if warning her soul, yelled, "Leave before it's too late. Get out!" She recognized those words and suddenly saw the glowing stack of library books piled neatly on the floor before her.

She felt something shake her. The dream continued. "Get out! Get out!" Bob yelled over and over again. Then something shook her again. She opened her eyes and stared at a man in front of her. At first, she did not recognize him.

"Christina, wake up!" Jason was growing frantic. "Are you okay? You fell."

"I'm fine," she mustered. But coming to, she realized that she was anything but fine.

"Did you trip and fall? What happened?"

"I don't know." She sat up, unable to stand, while she tried to comprehend what had just transpired.

"I heard you screaming, and when I came inside, you were on the floor." Despite his husky build and tough appearance, he could not hide his concern.

She stared wide-eyed at the gallery, shocked by the latest transition. Each and every painting had returned to its original state. The little boy, once again, happily played with the kittens. The milk had resumed its predictable white color. The newly married couple smiled sweetly at each other as their whole lives awaited, the bouquet boasting of brightly-colored roses picked in their prime, set off nicely by the white of the wedding dress. The elderly gentleman's kind smile had found its way back onto the painting, all evidence of an animalistic nature erased. The spiders had conveniently disappeared without so much as a trace. Not a single one remained anywhere to be seen.

"Their eyes," she started, pointing to the wall of inconspicuous paintings. "They were dark. They were watching me." But she felt silly even saying those words now that the paintings looked so innocent. "There was blood all over the floor! There were spiders everywhere…crawling on me. It was awful!" she shrieked, ready to do battle with what she had seen.

Jason looked under the table, beneath the chairs, and around the windows for signs of spiders or any bugs but found nothing. The room lied completely devoid of any evidence suggesting that anything abnormal had occurred. He wrapped his arm around Christina.

"Well, they're gone now. Probably means they've made their way up to our bed," he joked, giving her shoulder a pat. But she did not find it funny. She stood still, trying to make sense of what she saw and irritated that Jason would downplay the trauma of the situation. She had expected more support.

But then, a frightening possibility worked its way into her mind. What if she imagined the whole thing? Was she losing her mind?

Suddenly, Jason lifted his booted foot up in the air and stomped it down to the floor, breaking Christina away from her thoughts.

"Was this what you were afraid of?" Jason asked, a slightly amused look on his face as he took off his boot and turned it over, revealing a flattened spider. Christina jumped backwards. "Don't worry. This little fella's gone now." He walked towards a trash can that had been set up in the foyer while the men worked and scraped the boot's sole across the rim.

"You don't understand. They were everywhere." She stood, shaking, and seeing the fear in her eyes at the mere mention of what she saw, Jason realized his efforts to make light of the situation had been insensitive. He worried about Christina and did not like to see her so worked up. He felt certain there was an explanation for what she claimed to have seen but leaned towards the cause being fatigue and family stress.

He put his arm around her shoulder. "Let's get some fresh air."

"It's raining."

"It's just drizzling. Here, takes my umbrella if you want," he said, handing her an umbrella that had been sitting by the front door.

The two stepped outside and onto the front steps. The large amount of land surrounding the property was breathtaking. The sound of waves crashing off in the distance carried all the way up to the front of the house, reminding them that they were on an island lest they forget. A soft, warm summer breeze blew Christina's blondish-gray hair away from her face, revealing a stressed woman who could easily pass for middle-aged. Up until that point, she had been able to internalize her problems, hiding them away deep within her, but now they were popping up externally for all to see. Her forehead bore lines for the first time in her life, but the woman who once dreaded aging had not noticed, nor did she care. She felt lost in this place, and getting through the renovations was an effort similar to treading water; easy enough for short spurts but a test of resilience over the long run.

"Are you okay?" Jason asked bluntly as they walked towards the lawn. Christina refrained from making eye contact, looking away in the distance instead in an attempt to hide the tears. She was not used to feeling weak and hated to cry in front of others.

"I'm fine." She knew she was not but hoped hearing the words come from her mouth would be enough for Jason to leave her alone.

"I can tell you're not fine. You've become withdrawn. You barely eat and have gotten so thin." She had not realized up until that point that he had been so concerned about her. "Maybe it's time to leave this place behind. We can finish up here."

"I told you, I'm fine!" Christina insisted, her voice rising defensively. She had come to do a job, and by golly, she was going to finish what she started. She was not a quitter and needed this project. It had been so long since she had been able to do anything for herself, and no one…not John, not Jason, and not even dead Uncle Bob…was going to take it away from her, especially given how close renovations were to completion.

Jason took a deep breath. "But you're not fine. You just fainted from seeing something that only you could see." He hesitated, debating whether or not to say the next part. "I think something about this place is affecting you negatively, and I don't want you going through that any longer. It's not worth it."

"Do you believe me then?" She never could quite tell whether he was on her side or, like John, believed she was mentally unstable. Before he could answer, a strange sound drifted towards them. Both lifted and turned their heads in the direction of the noise. It was loud enough that it could not be ignored. The sound disappeared. Then another few notes aired, sounding like the product of a large organ.

Simultaneously, the two walked cautiously and with trepidation towards it, around the back of the manor and in the direction of the stone chapel. The afternoon sun was giving way to dusk, yet they could still see the stone building and the stained glass window clearly. A light shone through the window, revealing movement from within. As they approached, Jason extended his arm in front of Christina, moving her behind him for protection.

All of a sudden, Christina's ankle twisted beneath her. She stumbled forward, letting out an inadvertent yelp as she hit the ground with a hard thud. The music and movement within the chapel came to an abrupt stop. Had they heard her? Jason quickly helped her up.

"Look," he said in an urgent whisper. A quick scan of the terrain revealed a sight nearly as terrifying as a full chapel. She had seen them before. Holes, just like the ones dug by Ralphie, riddled the landscape. There were dozens of them, some large and others small, and there were even more off in the distance.

"I thought Sam refilled these," Christina said, her voice trembling.

"He did." Jason was sure of it. He had helped Sam carry the dirtbags over to the holes Ralphie had dug out, and the puppy had not returned to the area since. In fact, he had even mowed the lawn just hours earlier.

"Who's in there?" Christina asked, equally frightened by whatever was taking place in the chapel.

"I don't know, but I'm going to find out." The eeriness of the situation clearly disturbed him, despite his best efforts to remain calm and collected. He cautiously made his way up to the chapel, taking care to avoid falling along the way.

Jason pulled the double doors open slowly, peeked inside, and, after a moment, motioned for Christina to follow. The chapel was vacant, devoid of any living soul. Her rational mind begged her to run, but her curiosity convinced her to stay. The light emanating from the windows had dissipated and what remained was darkness, except for the last of the twilight and the oranges and reds it cast throughout. The pews, some rotting away and collapsing under the weight of the wood, sat empty, as did the space beneath them. The smell of rot remained heavy in the air around her.

To her surprise, there was no organ in the chapel. Although she had no recollection of one ever having been there, the undeniable sound of organ music emanating from the structure mere minutes before could not be disputed. Like the figures in the window, the music had seemingly vanished, leaving no trace behind except for racing hearts and confusion. Despite its visual emptiness, the room seemed very much alive.

"Let's get out of here," Christina said uncomfortably. Turning to leave, she caught a glimpse of a few objects sitting on the altar. "Wait a second. What are those?" They had not been present the last time she entered the chapel. The two walked past a few pews and towards the objects.

"My watch. I've been looking for this. What is it doing here?" Jason asked. He held it for a moment, examining it, as if unable to believe what he was seeing.

"I don't know. But look." There was something else. "A photo of the kids?" she asked, puzzled. She grabbed it and asked, beginning to panic, "How did this get here?" Like her grandmother's ring, something of importance had disappeared only to reappear on the altar, of all places.

He slipped the watch into his pocket and looked around, feeling the eyes of something unseen upon him. Christina felt it, too. The sickening feeling of being watched was overwhelming.

"We need to leave. Please, let's just go," she begged.

The two ran out of the chapel, stopping only to slam the doors behind them. It was dark now, and avoiding the holes was almost impossible. After a few stumbles along the way, they made it back to the manor, breathing a sigh of relief to have some distance, some barrier, between them and the chapel, although deep down, both knew it was not enough to protect them.

Once back in the attic, she and Jason sat in silence for some time, looking at the items they recovered from the chapel. While the watch appeared unscathed, the picture of the children had been burned along the edges for some unknown purpose.

"Have Sam and Jeremy noticed anything going on?" Christina finally broke the silence.

"I don't know," he replied. "They haven't mentioned anything to me." A distance seemed to be growing between Jason and the two other men, but she had carefully avoided breaching the topic, figuring he would discuss it when he felt ready. But viewing the lack of communication between them lately, she assumed that they had had some sort of falling out. "Have you talked to Annette about any of this?"

"I haven't told her," Christina shrugged. "And she never mentioned anything of this nature to me." She was starting to wonder how much Annette knew about the activity on the island…and how much she had been hiding.

She had the sudden realization that the events of the evening proved that the activity on the island was not all in her head. She had seen the fear and confusion in Jason's eyes as they experienced the inexplicable together, and knowing that she was not going crazy was of great comfort to her. But at the same time, it was no longer possible to dismiss strange occurrences as just a figment of her imagination. A strong desire to leave the island behind and never look back was overpowered by an even greater obsession with finishing renovations, the lure of only a few more weeks holding her hostage in a place she no longer felt safe, and she could only hope that the island would spare her the tragic ending of so many prior residents.

Chapter Nine

The days passed quickly as Christina buried herself in her work. She hardly noticed the nightly footsteps in the hallway or strange creaks and knocks along her bedroom wall as every ounce of focus was devoted to finishing the manor. But her work ethic was not the product of a desire to reunite with her children, rather a growing enchantment with the manor. It drew her in and beckoned her to stay, so forcefully that she could not break free of its grasp.

By the time repairs neared completion on the greenhouse, progress had come to a standstill. Five final glass panels sat waiting for installation, yet even walking towards the structure was an endeavor in of itself. She found herself wandering the massive halls of the manor, entranced with the old, intricate woodwork of the stairwells and the oil paintings of the dining room gallery. Some days, she would stand in front of the portraits, staring into the frozen faces of those who had lived there before her, wondering what their lives had been like, only to find upon breaking away from their grasp that many hours had passed. Other times, she found herself in the taxidermy room, looking at the deceased animals, petting their fur, and imagining them alive and out in the wild. What a strange fate, she thought, to end up in some dark room, invisible to the world. The work crew was so busy renovating two large bathrooms that they hardly noticed her absence. They expected that she was busy herself on the greenhouse or the gardening and did not question how she spent her day.

She found that she was no longer bothered by the shadows that moved out of the corner of her eye. It was part of the manor and had been there far longer than her, so what right did she have to question its presence?

One morning, as she stared emptily into a painting above the living room fireplace, undisturbed by its unnatural movement, as if performing a scene in a movie, the silence was broken by the ring of her phone. It had not rung in almost a week, and she jumped at the sound as she was suddenly shoved back into reality.

It was Annette. "Christina…are you there?" She had answered but was slow to greet her friend.

"I'm here," she said in a low voice that sounded as if she had just awoken.

"Sorry, did I wake you?"

"Oh, no. It's just been a little busy around here."

They briefly talked about progress on the manor and gardens, and Annette was thrilled to learn that the work was almost done. Despite her outward confidence in Christina, she had only half expected her to stick with the project and see it to completion.

"I bet you and the twins are ready to get back to normal life," she said. Christina had not told her that the twins were now living with John. She could not bring herself to admit, even to a close friend, that she was struggling to keep her life together. To her, it was a declaration of failure as a mother.

"It will be nice," she said agreeably.

"So where are you going to live? Have you found a new place?"

"I've been looking for a three-bedroom in Manhattan, but it's almost impossible to find anything for the next six months, so I'll probably have to branch my search out. Let me know if you hear of something." She was starting to regret having given up her apartment.

"Well, the old woman below me recently moved into assisted living, so I'll keep a lookout to see whether her apartment gets listed," Annette offered. "I'll ask around, too. I'm sure you'll find something, and you're welcome to stay on the island until it sells." It was a nice gesture, but in her heart, she knew she needed to leave and soon. "Actually, there are some potential buyers who have shown a great interest in the property. Granted, they have not taken a tour yet, but they were serious enough to pay a substantial amount for me to temporarily take the island off the market."

"That's wonderful. Do you need me to show them around?"

"No, they want to wait until the renovations are done. They heard through the grapevine about the chapel. It was not mentioned in the listing because I thought it would be torn down, but they absolutely love the idea of keeping it. Would you mind telling the crew to fix it up a little, just enough to sell? Like fixing the rotten pews and cleaning up the dust and debris. And open the windows to get that horrible smell out."

Christina struggled to comprehend the request being asked of her. The thought of even going near the chapel sent shivers down her spine. "Annette, you know I love you dearly and would do just about anything for you, right?"

"Of course."

"Well, I think you need to let the contractors tear it down."

Annette was silent for a moment, puzzled by Christina's request. "I'm sorry, what do you mean?"

"There's something wrong with it. I can feel it. And when you showed me the church," she hated to even call it that, "I couldn't help but notice that you felt it too." She hesitated to fully disclose what had been happening on the property, having already said more than she wanted to, but was shocked that Annette would even consider such a proposition given that her own uncle had taken his life in the building, although she still did not know that Christina had obtained that bit of information.

"I know it's not ideal. And yes, I don't like it myself, but if it helps me to finally be free of this property…please," she begged. "I won't ask anything else of you."

As a professional with a reputation to maintain, Annette would never admit to the horror she personally experienced on the island, yet the conversation convinced Christina that her fears were, in some way, justified. Still, she had a duty to help her friend prepare the property in any way necessary to sell. "Can I think about it?"

Annette was growing frustrated with Christina's lack of enthusiasm. "I'm sorry, but this just has to get done. Besides, the crew can do most of it."

"Okay, we'll take care of it," she reluctantly agreed.

"Great. Oh, I sent Mike out with some goodies for you and the twins. He should be there later this afternoon."

Annette quickly said her goodbyes. She had a lunch date in the city and needed to finish getting ready. Christina had no chance to discuss anything outside of the realm of what Annette wanted to know. Her personal struggles or feelings about the property were of low importance. She had become a hired hand, in Annette's eyes, and was there for one purpose only, and for the first time, she noticed how different their lives had become.

Talking with Annette brought Christina back into reality just enough to motivate her to complete the greenhouse. Working on a project took her mind away from the negativity of the property, even if just for a few hours, and she found herself actually enjoying the afternoon. Scrape, putty, set window, putty, repeat. It was easy enough, and the repetition had a calming effect. She was busy putting in new windows when Mike arrived, carrying a large paper bag in each arm.

"There you are! Busy, I see. Sam told me I'd find you out here." He looked at Christina, her blonde hair growing grayer by the day and knotted, as if she had not brushed it in weeks. Her face lacked makeup, and dark, puffy circles had formed under her eyes, now sunken and glazed. Deep wrinkles crouched into her forehead. Her baggy clothes hung loosely from her body, as if she were wearing someone else's oversized clothing, and it was evident that she had lost even more weight from the time he last saw her. She reminded him of a mental patient, and he wondered whether she was sick. He was deeply worried about the young mother, whose physical decline was so pronounced that she was nearly unrecognizable as the woman he met only a few months earlier. "Gifts from Annette," he said, handing over each bag. Then, with a concerned look, he asked how she was doing. "Thanks, Mike." She put the bags down beside her. "I'm fine. Just busy and trying to finish up a few projects. How've you been?"

"You know, same thing, different day. It's been a busy summer with all of the tourists in town, and ol' Stargaze is needing a tune-up, but I can't complain, to be honest. Where are the kids?" he asked, looking around. He had not seen them in a few weeks and missed them greeting him at the dock.

"Busy," she lied.

"Well, tell them I'll be back Thursday around two o'clock if they want to come out and say hi."

Christina could hold it in no longer. Tears began to stream down her cheeks. *Get it together*, she thought to herself, but the more she fought tears back, the more escaped. She had been able to push Charlie and Chelsea to the back of her mind for the most part, but the thought of them happily running around the island, greeting guests at the dock, reminded her of how quickly her life was unraveling. Her obsession with finishing projects and profound enchantment with the manor had consumed her every waking moment and nearly made her forget she was a mother at all. She had hardly noticed her physical decline, save for the occasional moments she would sigh in disappointment at the lack of clothing that fit.

"Is there something you want to talk about?" Mike offered.

It was times like this she missed her dad the most. Jason listened and helped as best he could, but nothing could replace the ear and advice of a father.

Before she could stop it, a divulgence of the inexplicable mysteries of the island and the torment she felt there came bubbling from her mouth, begging for someone to hear and help. She admitted to feeling watched by something evil that she could not escape, and she talked about the children…how her ultimate life fear of losing them had been realized, and how, at times, she found herself not even caring. He listened intently, not saying a word for some time. When it seemed that Christina was finished, he finally broke his silence.

"First of all, I believe you."

Christina felt relief, grateful that he did not think she was crazy.

"Second of all, I think you need to leave. As we discussed before, this island has a dark history, and I've lived in the Hamptons long enough to know only the lucky make it off intact." He started to say something else but caught himself as she took a step back, an angry look on her face. Her demeanor had abruptly changed from scared to infuriated.

"I can't…just leave. How dare you come here and try to get me to give up and leave. This is *my* island, *my* manor."

He was puzzled at the character shift, which served to confirm his suspicions of some sort of mental break. He reached out to grab her hands, and she pulled them back. The gall of some people, she thought. After everything she had done, everything she had sacrificed…her job, her social life, her kids…she was not going to sacrifice her role on the island.

And then, with a sudden meekness, "Please stop. It's all I have left." She slumped down to the ground and hung her head in shame at her situation.

"When was the last time you ate something?" Mike asked.

Her last memory of a meal was breakfast the morning before. She had not even thought to eat. Nourishment had seemed superfluous. Her sole focus had been on the manor, nurturing it, caring for it. She was its nurse. It was her patient. Her needs came second.

"Here, take this apple." He pulled an apple out of one of the bags from Annette.

Christina looked into the bags to see what else Annette had sent. One bag contained a few more apples, some dirty romance novels, and Sudoku books and was clearly meant for her. The other bag held a few children's books, one about turtles for Charlie, along with coloring books and crayons, card games, and stuffed animals. Christina cried harder, seeing the items for the kids.

"Sorry you had to see that," she said, wiping the remaining tears from her eyes. She chewed on the apple like a child, savoring each bite. It tasted sweeter than normal in her famished state. "Things haven't been easy around here."

"Listen, there's something you should know." Mike did not want to breach the subject of Albert again but felt he owed it to her to tell her the truth. "Do you remember me telling you about Jason and Jeremy's crewmember, the one who suddenly disappeared?"

"Albert. Of course. How awful that must have been."

"Yes, well, I only tell you this because I worry about you and think you deserve to know something he shared with me about this place. One night, Albert and I were talking, and he told me a fascinating story. He and the brothers had been replacing the drywall underneath a bathroom where a water leak had occurred…frozen pipes or something of that nature…when he heard his mother's voice calling from outside. His mother had died years before, but he was so certain it was her voice that he followed it. As soon as he got close to the voice, it traveled farther and farther away. He kept following it until he reached the chapel." When he mentioned the chapel, Christina could detect a bitter disdain for it in his voice.

Her body tensed, and the hairs on her arm stood straight up.

"Curiosity got the best of him, and he followed that voice inside. The chapel was empty, but then he began to notice movement and realized that the pews were, in fact, full of beings, I guess you could call them, dressed in black, sitting as if attending mass. He looked up at the altar at the front of the church and saw a coffin beside it. He felt compelled to look inside the coffin, and when he walked up to it, he saw himself lying dead in a suit with his arms crossed neatly over his chest. But what disturbed him more than anything was a carving on the body's right hand of a pentagram. As he turned to leave, he could see the faces of the beings, devoid of humanistic features. Their skin was reptilian, their mouths bared fang-like teeth, and their eyes were black and soulless. As he told it, he bolted out of there like lightning. He immediately left his job, one that he had loved for fifteen years, and never went back. A few days after he told me his story, he just disappeared. No one knows what happened to him or where he went. He just vanished, even leaving his belongings behind."

"That's so tragic." She wanted to disregard the story as an impossibility, just a scary ghost story, but because of her own experiences could not dismiss it.

"I'm sure the crew has seen things too. Anyone here long enough does." He paused briefly, as if evaluating whether it would be wise to continue, but seeing that Christina had calmed down, he continued. "I know a woman in town. We've been friends for years. She knows things. She can see and hear what others can't and has helped many of the locals with…disturbances. Would you like for me to have her reach out? Maybe she can help here."

"You mean like a psychic?"

"Yes. I would not recommend her unless I trusted her myself."

"Okay, you can give her my number."

"Her name is Robin Carlson. I will have her call you then. And if you decide you want to leave in the meantime, I will come and get you, even if it's in the middle of the night."

"Thanks, Mike. I appreciate that."

As he walked back towards the pier, Christina got the gut urge to follow, to leave the island once and for all. But, as if hands were reaching out and pulling her back, she found herself busily resuming her work on the greenhouse. A half hour later, she was putting the finishing touches on the structure and felt a sense of pride in having restored it to its original glory. She carried the bags from Annette into the house, made lunch for the three men and herself, cracked open a few attic windows to bring in some cool air, and laid down for a well-deserved nap.

She awoke an hour later to Jason stroking her arm, asking her whether she wanted to head over to their favorite beach area for fresh blueberries and wine.

"What time is it?"

"Five thirty. Sam and Jeremy left fifteen minutes ago, so it's just us. Oh, and Sam refilled the holes." Fixing the holes was becoming so commonplace that the absurdity of it felt diminished.

"Okay," she said, rolling into a sitting position. "Let me grab my shoes." She slipped on a pair of white tennis shoes that, over the course of working on the island, had become a brownish hue and walked the short distance to the water's edge.

Sitting on the beach, it was easy to forget the problems of the island. She buried her feet with only her toes visible above the sand. The sun was starting to set sooner, and she could see it sitting just above the distant tree line, as if suspended by an invisible string that would soon be cut to leave them in darkness.

Christina dreaded the evenings and the dimness of the manor. An electrician had come out the week prior, checked the electrical box and wiring in the home, and concluded that the electrical work was not a fire risk, at least. He explained that the older wiring was not designed to handle the current of modern-day appliances and that the only solution was to tear out all of the old wiring and replace it. But, doing so would not guarantee a fix, and he was unable to explain why the dimness persisted when no appliances were running. At the end of the day, nothing was repaired. He encouraged her to call back should she notice any power surges or flickering of the lights and left a two-hundred-dollar invoice on his way out. So it was left at that. The lighting remained dim and depressing, which, combined with the intense feeling of being watched at night, made her dread leaving the safety of her room for anything after dinner.

Jason gathered blueberries from the bushes while Christina sat, soaking up the warm breezes that drifted off the ocean's surface. Soon enough, summer would be over, and the manor would be complete. Normalcy was just around the corner.

Handing a handful of berries to her, Jason asked why Mike had stopped by. He had gone out to the dock to grab caulking inadvertently left behind by Sam and had noticed the two engaged in a serious conversation.

"He delivered a couple of things from Annette."

"You seemed upset. Is everything okay?"

"Yeah. I'm fine now. It's just a little hard not having the kids here, and some of the gifts were for Charlie and Chelsea, so…."

"I'm sorry. I know it's hard not having them here." He scooted over to wrap his arm around her. It was the most affection he had shown towards her lately. Both had seemed lost within the island's grasp, as if the waters around the property had swept them up into a giant wave and pulled them right under. He looked around briefly, seemingly afraid of being overheard. "But I'm glad they're not here. I see you suffering from this horrible place, as am I. Sometimes I worry we won't make it out…that we'll end up like the prior tenants. I feel like I'm going crazy."

His words frightened Christina, and she could see the fear in his eyes as he spoke. Something must have happened directly to him, she thought, and Jason quickly confirmed her suspicions. He confided that he had started to see spirits around the island on a nearly daily basis. There was the older couple walking hand in hand along the beach, the little children playing ball in the gardens behind the manor, a young woman in a maid's uniform carrying a bucket through the hallway, and then something much, much darker.

The week prior, he had been in the yard and saw a little boy, Charlie's age, walking along the manor's roofline. He seemed playful, bouncing a red ball along the roof's crest. Then the ball fell, bouncing merrily down the slanted roofline and towards Jason, who caught it in an inadvertent game of catch. Thinking that Charlie had returned unbeknownst to him, he yelled up to stay put and ran towards the door, hoping to reach the roof before anything happened to him. Just as he neared the front door, the boy jumped, falling hard to the ground below. Jason remembered yelling for Christina as he rushed over, but he stopped a few feet from the boy. His face looked green, scaly even, and the hand that stuck out from the shirt was no child's hand. Its long, thin fingers and brownish, overgrown nails, resembling claws, moved, tapping the ground. The body stretched, its torso and legs growing to the length of an adult's. It stood upright, hunched slightly, its red eyes staring intently at him. Jason took a few steps back, unable to grasp what stood before him. The creature followed his retreat, breaking into a full run towards him. Just when he thought there was no way to outrun it, it vanished before his eyes.

But it was not really gone. The creature was always around, taunting him, hunting him. There were times it would watch from the tree line or from one of the second-story windows as he worked outside. Other times, he would awake in the middle of the night to being choked, and despite his thrashes and screams, Christina never awoke to help him. He was terrified of these visions that only he could see and was beginning to doubt his own sanity. He had suffered in silence because no one, not even Sam and Jeremy, had seemed to share the sightings.

Christina admitted that she, too, felt the eyes of the creature watching her and never felt safe anymore. Her aloof behavior and physical decline had not gone unnoticed by Jason either.

"When Mike was here, I told him about everything, and he offered to have a psychic friend, a woman named Robin, come out and help. He said she would call me. Maybe she can help put an end to all of this, if nothing else, for whoever buys the place."

"What do we do until then?" The terrifying visions had become so bad that Jason found himself in constant fight-or-flight mode. "Maybe we should pray for protection." Christina was in agreement. One thing that bonded Christina and Jason was their Catholic faith, and although she did not truly expect anything to change as a result of prayer, she figured it could not hurt. Together, the two recited the Prayer to Saint Michael.

St. Michael the Archangel, defend us in battle; be our protection against the wickedness and snares of the devil. May God rebuke him, we humbly pray, and do thou, O Prince of the Heavenly host, by the power of God, cast into hell Satan and all the evil spirits who prowl about the world seeking the ruin of souls. Amen.

Both felt better after the prayer. And walking back to the manor later that evening, they felt a renewed sense of strength. The island seemed more peaceful. The flowers Christina had planted looked a little brighter, their colors bolder. The manor felt more inviting, and even the lights shone brighter. Christina wondered if the electrician had fixed the electrical issues after all, perhaps by jostling the wires during the inspection. The constant sense of being watched dissipated, and the island became a comfortable place to be for the first time since their arrival. Possibly, the prayer was all they needed. Christina's thoughts returned to her children, and she called them that evening, eager to hear their voices and find out how they were doing.

John answered the phone when she called. When he realized who was calling, he sighed.

"Hi, Christina," he said, taking care to avoid his pet name for her. "What do you want?"

She felt taken aback by his reaction to her. "I'd like to talk to Charlie and Chelsea." Their voices in the background carried over the phone line. The two were having a conversation about a card game they were playing.

Then she heard Rachel whisper disdainfully, "What does she want?"

A second of silence passed before he responded to Christina. "I don't think that's a good idea." He was still upset about their falling out at the manor, and her angry demeanor and disheveled appearance had cast serious doubts on her mental stability.

"Why not?" Christina asked, her voice rising.

He hesitated before answering but knew they would have to talk about the matter soon anyway. "Because you're not well."

"What do you mean I'm not well? That's ridiculous! Let me talk to the kids," she demanded.

He had not yet told her that he had, in fact, contacted their divorce attorney and informed him of her potential mental decline and asked for a mental health evaluation before the children returned to her care. He would tell her when the children were not present and reluctantly gave the phone to the twins, putting them on speakerphone so he could hear their conversation.

The children excitedly told her about all of the things they had done with John and Rachel. They had gone to the zoo, visited a water park, and taken a tour of their new school. When they mentioned a new school, Christina's heart sank. John had mentioned nothing of a new school, and she had already re-enrolled them in their prior school last spring. When she was done talking with the twins, she asked them to hand the phone back to John.

"What is this I hear about the kids touring a new school?"

John walked into another room and closed the door behind him. "Did you even realize that school starts all over the state next week? You're so wrapped up in your projects that you've completely forgotten about their school schedule."

"We're done here next week. Then they're going back to Saint Martin's and staying with me. What are you doing?"

He found himself unprepared to have this discussion, but here it was in front of him, needing to be addressed. "I have un-enrolled them. They will be going to our neighborhood school starting Monday." He continued, deciding it best to be honest with her about the return of the children to her care, "I spoke with Adam's law office, and they are going to ask a judge to request a mental health evaluation before they move back with you." As his words flowed out, devoid of emotion, she felt the gut-wrenching, sinking feeling of ultimate betrayal, as if she had been hit by a ton of bricks.

"What?" She could manage to say nothing else, and John suddenly felt a terrible sense of guilt over conveying the message that had to be given.

"Christina, look in the mirror. You are not well. This is the first time you have called the children in weeks. Charlie cries for you every night, yet that alone is not enough for you to give up your dream of renovating that place. You decided that stoking your ego and finishing a renovation was more important than him. And if that's not worse than my long trips away for work, I don't know what is. You did not even think to get your affairs in order in time for school to start." It was true, and she knew it. Her thoughts about the children lately had been minimal. "Have you even found a new place to live once you're done?"

She had not. She had tried but lacked the motivation to keep trying after a few potential apartments had not worked out. Each day melded into the next until a substantial amount of time had passed without any significant groundwork. Deep down, she knew John was right. She would have acted similarly had their roles been reversed. But a horrible resentment was growing towards him, nonetheless.

"I can't believe you're doing this." She had known Adam for years and felt blindsided by both of them. And this second betrayal from John was too much to bear. A sinister thought crossed her mind. Perhaps he wanted sole custody in order to receive parental support from her to fund a new life with Rachel. Or maybe he wanted to ruin her reputation among other attorneys just to twist the knife a little harder. "This isn't over," she vowed. "You can't take them away from me." But even as the words left her mouth, she wondered how she could have forgotten something as simple as her kids' school. How could she have let this happen?

"Don't you see? You've done this to yourself," John shot back. "Someone has to look out for them."

Immediately after getting off the contentious phone call and convinced that the day had nothing more to offer, she went to sleep, Jason by her side, his companionship more valuable than ever. She was thankful to have a sweet soul in her life, there for her when she needed someone the most.

In the middle of the night, she awoke and poured herself a glass of water, her body fighting to remedy the dehydration she had experienced from not eating or drinking normally. She sat in the living room of the suite, sipping the water through dry, cracked lips, the sensation of something cold in her belly foreign. The rhythm of Jason's snores was calming, and before falling back asleep, she watched the rise and fall of his chest and the innocent facial expressions that he made, similar to that of a child. But a moment later, she found herself struggling to recognize the man before her. Perhaps his skin had grown paler with the end of summer, or he had lost weight, too. She could not quite put her finger on it, watching him in the dark, yet something was different.

Chapter Ten

The next morning, Christina awoke early and went for a brisk walk, taking the scenic, one-mile-long trail around the island. Jason was still asleep when she got up, and she did not wake him. The conversation with John the night before was a bitter pill to swallow, and she needed some time alone to process her new reality. The first rays of sunshine along the shore promised a fresh start and the chance of a day better than the last.

Sam and Jeremy were already busily working on the chapel, carrying pieces of old, rotting wood to the burn pile and trash bags out to the barge. She would offer to help after her walk, she told herself. Though the chapel seemed to have taken on a more holy ambiance since reciting the prayer to Saint Michael…the stomach-churning stench had dissipated, and the heavy feeling of dread vanished…the memory of the evil that had so recently occupied the building lingered and sent a shiver down her spine.

The trail had remained clear except for a few newly fallen twigs here and there. The weed killer and fading summer had kept the weeds at bay. The calm water gently lapped against the shoreline as the sun rose to the east, and she could see a few boats off in the distance as the locals began their day. The sweet smell of roses filled the air as she passed the gardens, and she could see that the crew had gotten the fountain working again, its water sprouting happily from the top and cascading down its multiple levels to the bottom. If the twins were here, they would want to throw pennies into it and make a wish, she thought, feeling a twinge of sadness. The muddy pool was the sole neglected part of the property, a worsening eyesore that Annette continued to insist would be remedied soon by an outside company. In the distance, the greenhouse stool tall and proud once again.

"Can I get you all some coffee?" she offered as she completed her walk around the property. The men were standing outside of the chapel, and given that they had shown up early, she doubted they had had the chance to grab a cup before arriving.

"No, thank you," Sam declined.

"I'm alright. Thanks," Jeremy echoed. The two stepped back into the chapel. "We'll finish fixing up the pews and cleaning up some of this peeling paint later today," he said, running his hand over the wall. A chunk of old paint fell, cracking as it hit the ground. It was clear that the men had no interest in restoring the chapel in any way and were simply clearing it of debris to make it presentable enough to sell. "Honestly, there's really nothing you need to do in here." The news came as a relief to Christina. Despite its recent shift to normalcy, she wanted nothing more to do with the chapel. "But we could use some help planting a few bushes outside," he said, pointing to the barren landscaping along the side of the chapel. Although she preferred to not even be near the building, planting a couple of shrubs seemed minuscule compared to what the men had undertaken.

"You got it. You sure about the coffee? It's no trouble at all, and I have to make some for myself anyway."

"No, thanks. We're on a roll and want to be able to finish up in here today. We still have quite a bit of trash removal to take care of and some odds and ends to fix."

When she returned after coffee and breakfast, five boxwoods awaited along the chapel wall. The sun seemed brighter than usual, and the cool breeze made it ideal for heavier yard work. Feeling stronger than she had in weeks, she dug five large holes, evenly spaced, along the side of the building, the figure of Jesus watching from the stained glass window as she worked, which for the first time brought her a sense of peace. The sunshine stroked her face and bare arms, the brightness and warmth enveloping her like a giant hug. She had nearly forgotten what the sunshine felt like, as if her time on the island had been during a cold and dark winter. An enormous weight had lifted off of her shoulders, knowing that the men were on their final project. The end of this giant task…and nightmare…was finally near, and she would be getting back to her family very soon now, whether John liked it or not. He had no right to keep the kids from her, at least not until a judge ruled on the case, and she felt quite confident that any mental health examination would find her completely sane. She reminded herself that she was the attorney, and if anyone was going to win this battle, it was her.

She had just finished planting the last bush when her phone rang. It was a realtor in the Manhattan area letting her know that she had a three-bedroom flat available immediately, conveniently close to her old neighborhood and within budget. The realtor shared that the owners had suddenly moved back to their homeland overseas after a family member became ill and that the apartment was hers if she wanted it. Christina nearly jumped with excitement. This was her ticket away from the island and, from the description of the apartment given, a perfect home for the kids. In fact, it was close enough that they would be able to walk to school if they wanted to, after she re-enrolled them.

"Of course, I'll take it!"

"Just send the deposit by Friday then," the woman on the other end matter-of-factly requested and hung up.

To the realtor, it was just a day at the office, but to Christina, the unexpected surprise was like Christmas morning. What wonderful luck, she thought to herself. It was as though the universe understood that she needed a little extra help in that moment. She rushed off to tell Jason, searching the grounds to no avail. Perhaps he was working to remove remnants of the kitchen remodel from the basement. She went downstairs to check. A bright, cheerful kitchen with new cabinets and appliances and sparkling granite countertops sat empty, the lights off, leaving only the natural light from the egress windows. After a quick search of the remodeled bathrooms, she was just about to give up when she spotted Jason from a bedroom window, walking towards the manor from the dock. She ran outside to greet him, eager to share the news of her new apartment.

"Hey!" she said, waving as she ran in his direction. He waved back, smiling. She wondered if he had been carrying garbage bags to the barge for Sam and Jeremy. "Where have you been?"

"Oh, just doing a little shopping." She noticed that he had a grin that lasted a little longer than normal.

"You went into town? Why didn't you tell me? I would have gone with you."

"Oh, I just had a few errands to run and didn't want to bother you." Underneath his husky frame was a little kid fighting to hold back a giggle for a joke only he knew about. His smile was contagious, and Christina found herself smiling back at him. She could not quite pinpoint what it was but knew he was up to something.

"I have an apartment!" she blurted out, excited to share her own good news. "The realtor just called. There's one near our old neighborhood that just became available. The kids will each have their own rooms."

"That's great! When do you move in?"

"Well, next week, actually."

Christina and Jason had fallen in love, and neither wanted the relationship to dissolve once renovations ceased. The completion of Statham Manor presented a major decision to be made. They had discussed it during one of their visits to the beach as they nibbled on cheese crackers and drank wine. Jason had admitted that he wanted to be with her, wherever that was, but with that came the likelihood that he would have to leave behind the business he had started and grown with Jeremy. The thought of breaking away from J&J Contracting was made easier by the increasingly strained relationship with his brother. Jeremy no longer acknowledged his contributions and had gone so far as to stop including him in work discussions. It was as though Jeremy and Sam were the team now, and Jason was left on the outskirts.

Meanwhile, Christina desperately wanted to be back in the city. She knew that the kids needed normalcy, especially when so much around them was changing, and hoped Jason would make the choice to follow her.

"Well, I'm happy to hear that. See, everything works itself out," he said. "Hey, I'm pretty much done for the day. Why don't we go to the beach for a little while? We won't get many more chances. Someone will probably buy this place and turn it into a tourist destination, and that little beach of ours will be used to store canoes."

He was right. It would be one of their last chances to enjoy the beach. They walked hand in hand around the manor, past the chapel, through the woods, and to their secret spot. They had not brought any food or drinks this time. Their habit had always been to sit there in the early evenings, letting the stress of the day seep away with the receding waves. But now, as they sat in broad daylight, they realized that the beach had a completely different appearance in the early afternoon. The sands looked whiter, and the waves calmer. The tiny critters that migrated from the water to the shore in the evening were nowhere to be found, leaving a still landscape devoid of the movement they were accustomed to seeing. The sound of a distant boat could be heard before disappearing moments later.

They sat down and stared off into the water. Despite the island's problems, both had respect for it. They had grown here mentally, testing their respective limits as they beautified the old estate and its grounds. They had grown spiritually, too, as their faith in God was tested by the evil that resided on the land. And they had found each other and, for that, were grateful.

Jason pulled Christina close. "You know, before we met, I was lost. After my wife passed away, I never thought I'd find love again," he said, looking down. The pain of a loss so great could be read across his forehead. "I thought that chapter of my life had closed forever. And for years, I just accepted that my role was that of an uncle, a brother, a friend, and nothing more…until I met you. I remember seeing you for the first time and thinking that you were so beautiful. Then I met your kids and thought, they have a really good mom. I learned that you are a woman of talent and, in some mysterious way, can shape-shift between being a lawyer and a handyman. You are really something else. I love you and want us to spend our lives together. I want to live each day for you, Charlie, and Chelsea." Getting on one knee, he continued, "Will you marry me?"

He pulled a small, black box from his pocket and opened it, revealing a sparkly, pear-shaped diamond ring.

"Yes!" Christina yelled, stunned. "Oh my gosh, yes! I love you."

She stared for a moment at her hand, mesmerized by the ring's sparkle in the bright sunlight, and finally replied through tears, "I never thought I would find love again either." And it was true. When divorce proceedings had ended earlier that summer, she vowed that John would be the last. She was able to financially fend for herself and the kids and did not need a partner's monetary contributions. She also felt broken by betrayal and doubted she could ever trust another man again. But after meeting Jason, she learned that she did want a partner and, in fact, had not lost her ability to trust anyone besides John.

She curled into Jason's arms, noticing for the first time that he had worn cologne that day, not wanting to let go of that moment. He suddenly got a big smile on his face. He picked her up and swung around a few times.

"Jason! What are you doing? Put me down!"

But he had no intention of doing so. With one last turn, he had built up enough momentum.

"Let me…" But he tossed her into the water before she could finish, culminating in a splash. Then… "Why would you do that?" The water was chilly, certainly past peak swimming weather, and she was fully clothed. She scooped a wave with one arm and flung a heap of water in his direction. He laughed, took off his shirt, and jumped into the water with her. Surprisingly, it was the first time they had gone swimming at the shore.

"I knew you'd never get in on your own. And I figured we should take advantage of this private beach while we have it," he said, dunking his head under the waves and resurfacing with one of the many shells lying below their feet. "Peace offering?" he said, handing it to Christina. She grabbed it with an eye roll that gave way to a smile. She could not help but love his antics.

She had been wearing a blue dress with white flowers that were now soaked and weighing her down. She went back ashore and laid it on the sand before returning to the water.

A fish touched her leg as it swam past. It had been a while since she had swum in nature, and she had forgotten what it felt like to come into contact with other creatures.

"Follow me," Jason said, motioning with his arm.

"Where?"

"Just trust me. I have something to show you. It's not far."

"I don't know." The fact that at least one person had drowned in those waters made her hesitate, and she began to fear that a current would come in while they were in the water."

"The water's pretty shallow here." He started off away from the shoreline, Christina close behind, wading and occasionally swimming until suddenly the water became shallower, and a large sandbar appeared. It almost looked like a small satellite island out in the middle of an ocean.

"How neat is this?" Jason asked.

Christina smiled, sitting on the sandy surface. There were smooth rocks and pink and brown shells all around them. "This is cool! How did you know this was here?"

"Well, you know, when you've traveled these waters enough, you know where all of the sandbars are. I ran aground years ago before I knew the area well. Jeremy just about killed me for it. I've been careful about it ever since."

"He must have been pretty upset," she laughed. "How did you get the boat free?"

"Well, we had to push it off, but it took half an hour and scared us quite a bit." His smile revealed a fondness of that memory, and Christina wondered whether he and Jeremy were still on the outs. She had not seen them talk in weeks, and it was starting to concern her.

A twinge of sadness came over Christina as memories of her estranged sister, Eliza, came to mind, and she wondered whether the two would ever be close again. She had mourned that relationship over the years yet had grown to accept the solitude that followed, her need for sisterly companionship replaced by Annette.

Remaining were the fond memories of childhood, of holidays and birthdays as youngsters and sneaking out to parties as teenagers. But any lasting affection was snuffed out with the recollection of how their relationship devolved. Christina had told no one what had transpired, not even Annette, and she doubted she would even tell Jason. It was too painful.

It had been the week prior to her wedding, and Christina's schedule was filled with last-minute tasks. There was the final dress fitting, followed by a manicure and pedicure. The next day, she was supposed to stop by the florists to make a few last-minute changes to the floral arrangements. And a few friends had planned to take her out to buy a couple of outfits for her honeymoon the day after. She had left work early to get a head start on errands and, with a little extra time, decided to drive across town to a quaint little coffee shop near Eliza's home that they sometimes frequented together. Christina had fallen in love with its rustic charm and kind staff and called Eliza on the way over, hoping they could meet up, but no one answered. She reminded herself that Eliza was probably still at work.

As she walked towards the little shop, she could see a man and a woman sitting outside, but it was not until she got closer that she stopped in her tracks, recognizing the familiar face of her sister as one of the two. Although Eliza's hair was light brown and Christina's blonde, the two looked eerily similar and were often mistaken for twins. How perfect, she thought, but caught herself before impulsively running up to greet her when it became clear that she and the man were arguing. She could see only the back of his head but knew that dark hair from anywhere. She slipped behind the wall of the coffee shop, close enough to hear their conversation but remain out of sight.

"Well, are you going to tell her?"

And then, in a hushed tone, "Damn it, Eliza. She doesn't need to know. It was two years ago."

"You're getting married in a week. Is that how you want to start your marriage? Based upon lies?"

"We were taking a break. It's not something she needs to know about. Please don't say anything."

"I think she deserves to know who she's marrying." She sat with her arms folded, staring at the coffee and confections sitting before them.

"Telling her means we will both lose her. Why are you doing this? You're jealous, aren't you? Jealous that your younger sister is getting married and you're alone. Is that it?" he sniped.

She looked down, and John knew he had touched a nerve. It was old sibling rivalry rearing its ugly head. And then, with a sigh, "Okay, I won't tell her. But she won't make you happy. I give the marriage five years tops."

Christina did not wait around to hear more. She nonchalantly walked back to her car, playing and replaying the conversation in her head, wishing she had misheard but knowing that she had not. She mentioned her discovery to no one, not even John. Later that evening, when she asked how his day was, he talked about the training he had done at the airport all afternoon and how happy he was to be home after such an exhausting day. She knew he was lying, but at that point, the wedding was planned, gifts were bought, and guests were coming, and canceling would have been exceedingly difficult. And there was a reluctance to give up on everything they had built together. She would make it work with him. He would change after they got married. It would never happen again, she told herself.

However, the discovery of betrayal quickly led to the disintegration of her relationship with Eliza. After the wedding,

Christina cut off nearly all communication with her. And figuring that John had admitted to having a relationship with her, Eliza decided to keep her distance until Christina was ready to meet again, but that time never came. The day at the coffee shop became etched in her mind and created an insecurity in herself and her marriage, and she wondered whether that insecurity had doomed their life together from the start.

They sat in silence for a few minutes, each lost in their respective thoughts. The water seemed to grow colder and the waves stronger, and the sandbar had sunken to six inches below their feet. The tide was coming in, and Christina was beginning to feel nervous about being offshore.

"Let's go back," she begged.

The two quickly swam back to their private beach. A few crabs and sea turtles had made their way to shore as well, and once again, the sand had become a vibrant ecosystem, rich with movement as the creatures moved about. It was nearing dinnertime, and Christina's stomach rumbled. She would bake a lasagna that she had frozen the week before.

The two walked giddily back to the manor, arm in arm. Suddenly, all of the trials and tribulations cast upon them at Statham Manor seemed worth it. The door to the attic suite stood open, as if awaiting their return. Jason pulled her close and pressed his lips onto hers, slipping off the wet dress she had worn back in case anyone should see them. They felt at peace, as if the nightmarish events on the island had just been a bad dream.

Sam and Jeremy spent the following day on the mainland. There was a considerable amount of garbage that still needed to be disposed of, and dumping so many appliances and wood laden with lead paint had become a time-consuming feat for the two men, who drove from one garbage dump to the next, looking for a place willing to accept the refuse. Jason walked the property, tools in hand, fixing up odds and ends, while Christina completed the finishing touches on the garden, planting perennials around the fountains and in the gardens.

Every so often, she removed her garden gloves to adore her engagement ring. The one-carat pear sat on a plain gold band. Its simplicity and elegance were stunning, and she looked forward to showing it off to those she knew. The night before, as they lied in bed, Jason shared that he knew right after meeting her that she was the one. In fact, he had been so sure of it that he met with a jeweler only two weeks later. He had designed the ring himself, using gold melted down from his own mother's wedding band, and chose a pear because it symbolized the strength he knew their marriage would carry. When he finally picked up the ring, the jeweler had apologized profusely for how long the process took, but the length of time it took to create was of no bother to him. The ring was perfect.

The unexpected calm at Statham Manor made her a little sad to leave, but she looked forward to starting a life with Jason and reuniting with the twins. She would wait to share news of the engagement until they left the island. She wanted to enjoy that time together a little while longer before everyone found out. In a few short days, Annette would take a tour of the renovated manor and the gardens, and as long as she found everything satisfactory, the project would be considered officially completed.

The greenhouse looked better than she could have imagined. The men had hung several large ferns from the glass ceiling and built a few simple tables where she set out pots and garden tools to showcase their potential to buyers. She cleaned the windows, getting years of dirt and grime off the older glass so that light freely shone into the space, and rolled out a large rug that she had found in the basement. The once-dilapidated space had a renewed charm about it.

Jason surprised her with a basket packed with sandwiches and fruit slices. It was early afternoon, and neither had had time to eat lunch.

"Wow, this looks great!" he said, looking at the work Christina had done on the greenhouse. It looked like something out of a magazine. "I was planning to surprise you with a picnic in the rose garden, but maybe we could do it here instead."

"You like it? Check this out." She showed him some drawers she had installed underneath the tables using pieces from the old basement kitchen. "Plenty of space for storing garden scissors and dried seeds. Gosh, I wish I could take this whole thing with me. I don't know where I'd put it, though," she laughed.

"Well, maybe one day, we can buy a farm in the country and make a greenhouse that's even better than this one." Christina grew excited at the thought. She had always loved the idea of owning land, but her career path had warranted living in an urban area.

"With chickens and barn kittens? Charlie and Chelsea would love that." She unwrapped a turkey sandwich and began eating. "Do you ever wonder how life would be if your parents were still living? My parents have been gone for years now, but lately, I've missed them more than ever." The lack of extended family had been weighing heavily on her. She had had the realization that afternoon that her father would not be able to walk her down the aisle this time.

"I miss them every day. I miss Mom's crock-pots and fishing with Dad on chilly Saturday mornings. No one can replace them."

"You would have loved my parents. They were so happy together. A perfect match. I wish you could have met them." She knew that they would have thought highly of Jason but wanted them to wait longer before getting married. But she had dated John for years, and look how well that turned out, she thought to herself.

"If they were anything like you, I'm sure we would have gotten along just fine." He gave her a smile and quickly ate his sandwich, hungry after re-grouting an area of the bathroom floor that morning.

Bright sunlight streamed through the ceiling, warming up the room to the point that Christina opened the door to let fresh air in. She could see a dark cloud in the distance, but otherwise, it was a perfect day. The breeze felt nice, and the two opted to open a bottle of wine before heading back to the manor. Christina still had dusting and decorating that needed to be finished before Annette's visit.

By early evening, the storm cloud that had been so far off was making its way to land. Thunder rumbled not far offshore, and flashes of lightning brightened the darkness that seeped into the early evening hours. Christina and Jason sat in the attic suite, listening to the pitter-patter of rain against the rooftop. It was relaxing. Christina made hot chocolate and brought out a pack of chocolate chip cookies, and the two sat, watching a movie, before falling asleep on the sofa.

A few hours later, both awoke with a jolt to a loud bang. Christina thought it was just a loud clap of thunder and quickly fell back asleep, but Jason could not so easily disregard what sounded like a large mirror falling and shattering. He decided to look around, just to be sure nothing was amiss. He wandered from room to room, finding all to be normal. No mirrors had fallen, and every window and door remained tightly closed and locked. The house looked exactly as it had before they went to sleep. He resigned himself to returning to the suite but found himself waking every hour or so, unable to dismiss the strange noise as mere thunder.

Chapter Eleven

The noise the night before was easy enough to dismiss as thunder or a fallen branch. Christina had nearly forgotten about it by morning and awoke feeling fully rested and refreshed. Jason lied beside her, finally asleep after a restless night. Donning her white robe, she walked over to the kitchen and put on a pot of coffee. While it was brewing, she would walk around the house for a quick look just to be sure, hoping to dispel any concerns Jason had during breakfast.

The old oak staircase beckoned her with its intricate carvings, and Christina found herself running her hand along the woodwork, drawn in by the artistic creations of craftsmen long ago. The carved town spanned the wall, and she recognized one of the structures as Old Hook Mill. Surrounding the mill were the older houses of East Hampton, still standing during her last visit, as if immune to the passage of time. Waves indicated where the water stood, its space denoted in soft swirls. And across the water was Statham Manor, easily enough recognizable by its fountains and chapel. Five men gathered around a fire in the courtyard. She wondered who they were…possibly members of the Statham family or a tribute to the Natives who once resided on the land. The carvings had an energy about them that drew her in closer, entrancing her, and it was several minutes before she completed her descent.

Outside, she was greeted by the cool freshness of a late-summer morning and breathed in deeply, feeling a sense of reinvigoration and excitement for the day ahead. The storm had left minor debris along the brick drive and green fields, mostly along the tree line. So far, so good, she thought to herself. There did not appear to be any fallen trees, and the windows and roofing along the front of the house had been spared from damage. But as she approached the greenhouse, she stopped in her tracks. The sight before her was so incomprehensible that, for a moment, it did not quite register what she was seeing.

The greenhouse, or rather lack thereof, was gone, as if it had vanished into thin air. She stared in the direction of the absent structure she had worked so hard to restore, only to see the trees behind it. She blinked and looked again, expecting to see what surely must be there, only to find emptiness. She ran over, heart pounding, still believing that some trick of the light was at play, but as her steps grew closer, she noticed piles of broken glass and wood beams where the greenhouse once stood. Along one of the edges of debris sat a corner of the rug she had brought up from the basement the day prior. A plant still hung from one of the fallen beams. But without knowledge of what the structure had been, it was difficult to distinguish from an inconspicuous pile of building refuse that one might see on any construction site.

She buried her head in her hands and cried. It was as though someone had stolen something from her, and she could not help but draw comparisons to the vegetable garden that had rotted away mere hours after completion.

She was still in tears a few minutes later when Sam and Jeremy arrived.

"What happened?" Jeremy asked, stunned by what lied before him. "Are you okay? Did you get hurt?"

"I'm okay," Christina finally mustered. "I don't understand how this happened. There was a loud crash last night during the storm, and then I found it like this."

Sam walked cautiously around the old greenhouse, inspecting the remains. "I don't see any burns, so I don't think it was lightning. And there's obviously no fallen tree. I wonder why it collapsed."

It was a mystery. Christina had had the men check the structure before she replaced the windows, and the foundation had been sound. She caught Sam and Jeremy looking at each other, as if a silent conversation was going on between them, but neither said anything aloud.

"What is it?" she asked, curiously. "Do you know something?" Sam looked away, as if he held a secret he was not supposed to reveal. "Jeremy?"

"We checked the structure ourselves not two weeks ago, as you remember, and everything was fine." Jeremy hesitated, as if unsure whether he should continue. "We've had a lot of issues ourselves on this property, things that cannot be explained…tools going on by themselves, strange knocking on the walls, your vegetable garden, and now this." He looked around, as if he knew he had said too much. She wondered if he had the feeling of being watched, too. "All I can say is I'll be happy to finish up here."

"Don't worry about the mess. We'll get it cleaned up," Sam offered. "But you might want to warn Annette about this before her visit. I wouldn't want her coming here unprepared to see it missing." The men had quite a few odds and ends on their list that day and left the cleanup for later.

Christina went back inside to find Jason, who, blissfully unaware of what had transpired outside, was cooking bacon and eggs.

"Honey, what's wrong?" he asked when he saw her face, putting down the spatula.

"The greenhouse…it's gone," Christina struggled to hold back tears. "It completely collapsed in the storm. Nothing's left."

"You're kidding," he said, looking shocked. "Well, we can fix it." His optimism usually brought a smile to her face, but today, it only deepened her sorrow.

"There's nothing *to* fix. Go take a look."

Jason walked towards a window facing the former greenhouse and could not believe what he saw. "Jeez, I knew something broke last night, but…that?" He suddenly wondered why he had not thought to check outside and was sorry Christina had been the one to find it in shambles.

"It's crazy, isn't it?" Christina quickly dressed and then walked to the living room to sit and digest everything that had just transpired when a knock came from the front door.

"I'll get it," Jason offered. "Jeremy or Sam probably just locked themselves out again."

"No, you finish breakfast. I'll take care of it," Christina offered. She descended the stairs for a second time that morning, annoyed that the men would be so careless as to lock the door behind them. Her hand ran along the carvings on her way down, and once more, she felt herself drawn to the town, studying it, touching every peak and crease, and observing every bump. She imagined the carpenter busy at work, pouring his heart and soul into each detail, working day and night until his masterpiece was done. And for a brief moment, there was the visual flash of the cloaked figure walking the staircase and halls of the manor. She saw visions of others, too, some in period clothing, others looking a bit more modern, all with the blank stare of death in their eyes. She jumped back, and with the release of her hand, the hold over her was broken and the visions ceased.

Again, there was knocking, this time more insistent. "Coming!" Christina shouted, but after a step towards the door, she felt herself drawn to the dining room photo gallery. The occupants' eyes followed her every move, as if begging her…willing her…to understand their collective pleas to leave Statham Manor.

The knocking had given way to pounding. She could hear Mike's voice asking if everyone was okay. Suddenly snapping back into reality, she rushed through the foyer and opened the front door.

"Hi, Mike. Sorry, I wasn't expecting you. Come in."

"Is everyone okay? I saw that the greenhouse collapsed. I've been knocking for fifteen minutes."

"Fifteen min…?" Had it really taken her fifteen minutes to descend the stairs? "We're all fine. There was a nasty storm last night, and it just collapsed. Horrible, isn't it? Perhaps it was the strong winds we've been having." But both knew deep down it was not. Surely, Mike could not have seen the greenhouse from the shore. Why was he here, she wondered?

As if responding to her thoughts, he asked, "Remember that woman I told you about?"

"The psychic?"

"Robin…yes. I brought her with me today. She called me this morning and asked that I bring her out right away. She said it was urgent. Sorry for the lack of notice."

"That's okay. Where is she?"

"She's walking the property right now. She wanted to see if she picks up anything on her own before talking to you."

"Mike, I have to tell you that we may have already gotten rid of whatever was on the property ourselves. Jason and I said a prayer to Saint Michael the other day, and everything seems to have been peaceful ever since. So I don't really think we need her. I mean, I would hate to waste her time, is all."

"You did this the other day?" Mike asked, seemingly surprised. Before Christina could answer, a pleasant-looking woman in her mid-sixties appeared from around the house. She had curled her short, gray hair that morning as she always did on days that she left the house and chosen a soft, white blouse, which was tucked neatly into her gray trousers. She wore a pair of shiny black flats with buckles on the top. Her dressy attire was the antithesis of Christina's cutoff jeans, worn sweatshirt, and sandals. Mike could not help but notice that, despite their age difference, their graying appeared identical.

"I'm Robin," she said, extending her hand.

"Christina."

"Lovely place this is. You've done a nice job fixing it up. It looks nothing like it did the last time I saw it."

"You've been here before?" Christina was intrigued.

"Yes, some years ago. I was an acquaintance of the prior owner."

"You knew Bob?"

"I did. We worked on the force together for many years. He was an outstanding officer."

"Are you an officer, too?"

"No, but I helped him with several murder cases, my role being that of a psychic medium. Whenever the team ran into a dead end on a case, if they had no clues and just needed a direction to go in, I would visit crime scenes with them and share my findings. Ever since I was a little girl, I've had the ability to see and feel what others cannot…people who have passed on, tragic events…but my true gift is being able to help others with it." She smiled warmly at Christina, studying her for a moment.

Mike turned to Christina. "Robin's been a godsend for several police departments and has been vital to solving how many crimes now?" he asked.

"Oh, I don't keep track any longer," she said humbly.

"Well, she is aware of what you've been experiencing here and, hopefully, can help," he went on.

Robin placed her hand on Christina's shoulder. "There is nothing to worry about, dear. I'm not here to judge, just to assist in any way I can. Believe it or not, I have experienced many things myself on the island, and I understand what you are going through." Her tone was understanding, motherly, and had a gentleness about it.

"I do appreciate you coming all the way out here, but like I told Mike, things seem to have calmed down since reciting a prayer to Saint Michael the other day asking for protection. I don't know that there is anything left to fix, honestly. The days since the prayer have been so quiet. It's been, dare I say, pleasant."

"I noticed a heap of glass and wood off to the side of the house," Robin said bluntly, now with an expression of concern. "The greenhouse, if I'm remembering correctly. What happened?"

"You're the psychic. You tell me," Christina joked, but neither Mike nor Robin laughed. She cleared her throat. "It fell last night during the storm. We had a lot of wind, and I guess it just blew over." She knew better, though. It had not…could not…have just blown over, but there was no other logical explanation for it.

"Have you felt anything different since it fell? Or noticed that things seemed a bit off?"

Christina's first impulse was to stubbornly deny any change, to re-emphasize that things on the island were normal. But as she opened her mouth to speak, the words did not come out. How long had she spent mesmerized by the staircase woodwork and picture gallery that morning as Mike awaited her? She confessed to Robin her sudden, renewed entrancement with the manor but admitted that, although strange, she did not believe it was proof that anything was wrong. Robin listened intently and did not seem surprised by what she said.

"Do you mind if I walk the manor by myself? It will take fifteen to twenty minutes. I would like to do it alone, if you don't mind."

"Of course," Christina said, gesturing with her right arm towards the door.

Christina suddenly realized that Jason was still upstairs, probably waiting on her to come up for breakfast and definitely not expecting company. How long had he been waiting? She felt a sense of relief when she saw him walk up behind them and wondered how he had managed to get outside without being seen.

He greeted Robin with a hi, and she returned his smile.

"Robin, this is my fiancé, Jason."

An uncomfortable amount of time passed before she responded, to the point that Christina almost interjected. "Pleased to meet you. I hope you don't mind my coming unannounced. I am a friend of Mike's and a psychic medium. He gave me a brief summary of some of the unexplained events plaguing the island, and I am here to help provide some help." As she talked, she stared intently at Jason. Christina did not think she had blinked at all since she laid eyes on him. Turning to Christina, "Just give me a few minutes, dear," and she walked through the front door. Mike had wandered over to the site where the greenhouse once stood and was looking down at the remains, searching for clues that might reveal how the beautiful, old structure met its fate.

"What was that all about?" Jason asked Christina in a hushed voice.

"Remember the woman Mike was going to send out? Well, that's her."

"She seems a bit odd," Jason said in a low voice. "And we already took care of whatever was here," he added.

"I know. But Mike said that she had a bad feeling about the property and asked him to bring her out right away. That's why they're here."

"It's not our problem in a couple of days. I don't think she needs to be here, and I don't want her stirring something back up."

"I guess if there is something left over though, it would be better to get rid of it now before the new owners come in," Christina postulated.

"I guess," he conceded. "But no spells or witchcraft. I don't want to be a part of anything like that. She can say more prayers if she wants or tell us what she knows about the property, but that's it."

She was surprised by his reaction to having Robin there. He was not the type to leave a problem for another person. She had known him to always be concerned about helping others.

Mike returned to the couple. "Looks like there's another storm coming in." Both Jason and Christina had been so preoccupied with the unexpected visit that neither had noticed as the few rays of morning sunshine slipped ominously behind gray clouds, a darkness overtaking the island. "I'm going to head back to the ferry and wait out there. I've got some paperwork that needs to be done by this afternoon."

"You're welcome to come inside," Christina offered. "There's no need to stay out here."

"No, but thanks anyway. The covered area of the ferry stays pretty dry. And besides, this visit is between you and Robin. If you would, let her know I'll just be waiting for her out there," he said, looking in the direction of the dock. It was obvious he did not want to be around for whatever she had in store.

"Okay," Christina replied. She thought it odd that Mike preferred the ferry, given an approaching storm. "If you change your mind, we'll leave the front door unlocked."

Christina and Jason looked at each other and shrugged their shoulders as he walked off.

A few minutes later, Robin completed her walkthrough of the house, and the two joined her in the foyer. Christina was hoping it would be a quick visit. Maybe the psychic had some sage to burn or a few more prayer recommendations and would be off on her way. If the visit was fairly quick and the storm held off, Christina could help the crew make quite a bit of headway in the greenhouse cleanup. She wanted to at least be able to tell Annette the mess had been taken care of when she informed her of the collapse.

"Come sit with me." Robin motioned for Christina and Jason to follow her into the formal living room. The sofas sat waiting, luring them into luxurious comfort. The marble fireplace and the original oil painting above imparted a sense of grandeur. Despite residing in the manor, it was one room that they never used for themselves, finding its ostentatious design somewhat off-putting. They much preferred the simple living room of the attic suite for relaxing. "You two might be wondering why I came out here so unexpectedly."

"Well, to be truthful, I think all this hocus pocus might be a waste of time," Jason responded bluntly. Christina gave his leg a light kick and imparted a brief side glance, as if to warn him to knock it off.

"What he means is that we just aren't sure we need any help. Like I said before, the island has been so calm since we said our prayer."

"I understand your concern. And I promise, I am here only to help. I am not a witch and do not cast spells or anything of the sort. Just someone with a gift to see and talk to those who have passed on. I can also sense what has happened in the past and, very occasionally, the future. And I find that when I see what has not happened yet, the situation is the most dire. To be frank, that is exactly why I'm here. Last night, I was visited by the spirit of a young woman who once lived on the property…a nanny of several children, I believe. She showed me visions of her life working for a wealthy family and of the evil that currently inhabits the island. She warned me that this evil sees you as its next victim and that if I do not intervene immediately…and I know this sounds dramatic…you might not make it out alive." Looking directly at Christina, she continued, almost in a whisper, "It's watching us now. Can you feel it?"

Christina felt it, too…a certain heaviness that had encompassed the island since her arrival. She felt the extra set of eyes boring deep into her soul. And then, in a panic, she stood up from the sofa and took a few steps back. Her voice rose. "Stop. Just stop. Why are you doing this? We cleansed the property, we prayed to Saint Michael the Archangel, who is protecting us and has barred all evil from the property. We have been fine ever since. Whatever was here is gone."

"My dear, I wish it was so, but it is here, and it is stronger than ever. It has just been in hiding. But it *is* back, and you are in danger. You must leave this place immediately."

"Then why, after so much torment, have things been so calm?" Her voice was quieter, as if relenting after a lost battle.

The medium continued, "Your prayer reigned in the evil temporarily, but it is more powerful than you can imagine. The nanny…she showed me carvings, the ones along the stairwell. You've been entranced by them, finding it hard to pull yourself away, haven't you?"

Christina nodded.

"And perhaps drawn into your renovations…excessively, should we call it…to the exclusion of that which matters most to you in life…your children?"

Again, a nod to the affirmative.

"Your obsession with the manor, the carvings, and the paintings is this evil force. It is luring you in, trying to make you worship it. It wants your soul."

"Forgive me for asking, but how do you know this?"

"There is going to be a lot I share with you that I cannot prove. I just ask that you keep an open mind and understand that I would not be here this morning if I didn't think this was a matter of the utmost urgency," she reminded Christina and Jason. "How much do you know about the history of the property?"

"We visited the historical society in town a few weeks ago and did a little research. A wealthy George and Elizabeth Statham built the house in the late 1800s and hosted extravagant parties before it was eventually sold and transitioned into an orphanage during the war. Then there were the series of couples who tried to renovate the manor as part of business ventures. We also learned about many unfortunate deaths, some of them children."

"Very good," Robin replied, impressed with Christina's knowledge of the property. "You have done your homework. The Statham's were the original couple on the island. They were a golden couple amongst high society, you could say. They had it all. They had youth, beauty, money, and fame. The most exclusive parties were hosted here, including several extravagant fundraisers for various charities. There were fancy balls and, on some occasions, even live lions and elephants shipped in for sideshows. In the 1880s and 90s, this was the place to be. But then, things changed. George's oil company had several financial setbacks, and the Statham's risked losing their livelihood and status as part of society's elite if things did not improve. It is rumored that one of their party guests spent the night after one of the gatherings, talking over cigars with George about a "secret weapon" for success that only a handful of the luckiest and wealthiest men in the world were privy to. He convinced him that he could regain his success and wealth if he took a step back from his Catholic faith and worshipped the ancient deity of success, Ganesha. Elizabeth was initially reluctant to the idea of worshipping false gods but, as their fortune began to dwindle, became desperate.

That Fall, the profits at George's oil business doubled. Stockholders eagerly purchased more shares, and by the following Spring, oil production was booming. A year later, the value of his company doubled once again. Business continued to grow, and with the renewed success of the company came, obviously, more wealth and notoriety amongst the highest in society…but also fear of losing their renewed prosperity. Soon, the couple was searching for any God, good or bad, to help them further broaden their success. It became an addiction that ultimately led them to worship the evilest of all gods. The couple began practicing black magic in their once-holy chapel, and a group of followers…wealthy doctors, lawyers, and businessmen from all around New York…joined them, eager for a taste of the Statham success. But there was a steep price to pay to the false gods, who required the steady sacrifice of innocent victims. Employees of the Statham's, and even business acquaintances, started to mysteriously disappear, and no one ever knew what happened to them. And in the process, the Statham's inadvertently opened a doorway to the other side…the realm of the dead…allowing evil onto the land. As this evil grew in strength, so too did its thirst for death. I believe that at some point, it began to hunt victims on its own accord, leading to numerous drownings and suicides over the years."

The storm grew nearer. A flash of lightning illuminated the room, and a loud clap of thunder followed.

"Does that have anything to do with what we've experienced…the feelings of being watched, seeing that cloaked figure?"

"Yes. The evil has not gone away and probably never will. It just goes into hiding now and then, but it's always here, just waiting for the right opportunity to strike. The cloaked figure…a demon…has been preventing those who perished on the island from finding peace and moving on. They are here because there is no place else to go." She paused for a moment, as if evaluating whether to continue. "Dear, they are the faces in the picture gallery…a trophy walls of lost souls."

Christina was quiet, and then she shared something that she had not told anyone. "I've been seeing Jason and myself in one of those paintings. At first, I thought I was just seeing things…but I'm quite sure of what I saw the other night," she said frightfully. Several nights before, she had noticed a new painting in the dining room gallery. When she had leaned in to examine it, she was shocked to recognize the location as the shore where she and Jason liked to sit and talk at the end of each day. Just as soon as she realized what she was looking at, two people had appeared within the painting, sitting arm in arm with a picnic basket to the side. That had sent her running up to the attic. She no longer doubted anything Robin was telling her. "What do we do?"

"You are in grave danger and must leave now. I'm sorry, but there is no other way. But before we leave, we must help the other victims to move on. Their bodies remain on the land, and they want to be found. Only then can their spirits cross over to where they belong."

"I've worked all over the island and have not seen any gravestones."

"They're not marked, my dear, but you know where they are."

Christina sat back in her seat, quietly realizing that she knew exactly where the graveyard was.

"Jason, grab a shovel." Robin looked at her wide-eyed. The two sat quietly until he returned, and together, they walked to the green field behind the manor, lightning flashing ominously around them. Despite everything that had happened, Christina was doubtful that anything would be found but felt that it was worth validating anyhow. Jason began to dig in the same spot that Ralphie, the little puppy, had dug twelve rectangular holes. After half an hour, the rain drenching his clothes, he handed the shovel over to Christina while he took a break. The ground had become a muddy mix of dirt and leaves, making progress much more difficult.

It was not long before she heard the clanking of her shovel against something hard. The island was riddled with stones, and she assumed that to be a major reason the manor had been built of the material. She scooped away mud by hand, trying to grasp how large the stone was so that she could dig around it. It spanned the entire width of the hole. She dug on either side, wiggling and pulling at it, until it came free. It was not until she set it down and brushed it off that her worst fears were confirmed. Her nursing background made it easy enough to identify the "stone" beside her as a human femur. She looked back into the hole, now larger after removing the object, and was horrified to find more bones.

Robin did not seem surprised and simply nodded, a sad expression on her face at the discovery.

"Oh my God," said Jason when he realized what they were dealing with. "You were right. How did you know?"

"They showed me," Robin responded. "There are dozens of them. Twelve in this plot and many more around the island. You have been living in a graveyard."

Christina looked apprehensively at the little chapel that appeared so innocent to the unaware. "How strange that all of this took place here…that what was the godliest part of the island became the most unholy," she pondered aloud.

No sooner had the words left her mouth than the chapel came alive with the sound of music and chanting. Light shone through the large stained glass window of Jesus leading the sheep, and behind the window, there was movement.

"What the hell," Jason stated slowly, softly, unsure of what he was witnessing.

Christina stared in horror, mouth agape, watching as tall shadows moved within.

Unable to refrain from seeing firsthand the events taking place inside, Robin approached the chapel doors, pulling them open. Christina and Jason followed closely behind, desperately wanting to run but knowing they had a duty to protect Robin. They stopped just beyond the threshold, paralyzed in fear by what lied beyond.

Men, women, and children, dressed in period clothing, filled the pews, eagerly listening to a sermon given by the cloaked preacher, the bumps of its reptilian skin visible even from its position behind the candlelit altar. The men wore older-style suits and the women full dresses with petticoats, their long hair neatly pulled up into bonnets. No one seemed to notice the new guests until one of the men turned his head and faced their direction. Then another and another turned until all eyes were upon them, and the voice at the front stopped speaking. Pure silence followed, the room devoid of even the sound of breathing.

Then came the sound of dripping, as if a pipe were leaking onto the floor beneath it. Christina noticed the slightest movement out of the corner of her eye. At first, she thought it was a cockroach crawling down the wall but when she looked more closely, saw rows of dark red appearing from nowhere, viscous and heavy, streaming from ceiling to floor in fine, vertical lines. More streaks formed until nearly the entire wall was the red of a freshly fallen autumn leaf. The smell of iron and decay overpowered the room, leaving little room for denial of what lied before her.

"Join us," came the deep, raspy voice of the preacher. He stared directly at the trio. Christina's heart was racing as they backed out of the large double doors and into the yard outside.

"What was that?" Christina shrieked.

Robin stood calmly, silently, her fear hidden behind determined eyes. Jason and Christina could see her take a deep breath as the churchgoers poured out after them. Her lips muttered something inaudible.

"Join us!" a kind-looking lady wearing a hoop skirt and pearl earrings begged.

"Yes, join us!" said a man in a suit, holding out his arms. The little boy next to him gave a sweet smile that began to stretch unnaturally upwards at the corners, blood dripping from either end and down his chin. His eyes rolled back into his head, leaving only the whites visible, and he let out a horrendous, inhuman laugh. The woman in the hoop skirt looked different, too. Broken capillaries dotted her face, and her head bent unnaturally to one side, as if she had been hanged. The gentleman's head was bloodied, and appeared to have been severely injured by a sharp instrument, a large gash visible along the backside. A few feet away, a little girl in a dress carried a doll with her unsevered arm, while a bloodied stump occupied the other. Two men in identical suits foamed at the mouth, their eyes bloodshot. One by one, they walked into the field, vanishing before their eyes.

A low rumbling of what felt like an earthquake shook the island. The trees swayed, and thump after thump could be heard as the weakest fell. The ground divided and sank below them, pulling Jason down with it. As he scrambled back up to the surface, he realized that his foot was stuck on something. He bent over to free it, expecting to find a root, and was horrified to discover that it was not a root, but a skeletal hand, that pulled his foot, its long, brown nails digging into his skin, refusing to let it free from its grasp. A skull watched, amused, as he fought to escape, its eternal smile seeming to mock his struggle. Christina took the shovel and hit the bony hand, releasing Jason from its grasp. He made one last push out of the grave and onto the ground above.

But there were others. Surrounding them was a field of dug-out graves, some grouped together and others far apart. They were deeper than the last time, revealing the remnants of dozens of victims, long forgotten to the world.

A dark shadow moved along the tree line. Jason noticed it first, its red eyes piercing and evil. It moved angrily towards them at a fast-walk pace.

"Run!" Robin ordered. The trio sprinted back to the manor until they could figure out what to do next. Jason slammed the front doors shut behind them, securing the locks tightly, yet they all knew it could not keep out what was there. They sat around the dining room table for several minutes, catching their breath and listening to Sam and Jeremy working on something in the kitchen below, blissfully unaware of what had just transpired.

"Those poor people never made it off Statham," Robin lamented. "But I have released them from the grasp of that creature, and they are free to move on. However, doing so has angered the evil exponentially. It is too strong for me to fight."

The thunder had become much louder. The lights of the manor had resumed their dimness and were duller than ever, to the point that Christina simply turned the lights downstairs off in favor of what remained of natural light. The manor had taken on a far more ominous presence just in the short time they were outside, and it was clear to all three that the evil of Statham Island had returned, only more dangerous and powerful than before.

Chapter Twelve

The trio sat in the dining room, waiting for the heavy storm to pass. It was impossible to sail in the rocky waters, and they had no choice but to remain until conditions improved. Christina made sandwiches for the group, her hands still shaking as she spread peanut butter and jelly across the bread. The simple, familiar task helped to take the edge off her anxiety and the fear of what could come next. As she ate, she found herself walking the floor, peering out of the windows, expecting nothing less than to find the churchgoers roaming the property in a zombie-like state, plotting their entry. Yet there was complete normalcy. Even the graves had refilled on their own accord, and the grass looked just as it always had.

Christina had just taken another bite of her sandwich when she noticed something peculiar. Across from her sat the painted portrait gallery. She was very familiar at this point with each picture…the hairstyles, the clothing patterns, the facial expressions…given her fascination with the gallery wall. She stared at the paintings daily, drawn in by them. And yet, the pictures had once again morphed. Several sets of eyes now stared upwards, as if in a collective eye roll. She looked away, thinking the shock of what had just transpired was making her own eyes play tricks on her. Yet when she looked again, their eyes remained fixated on the ceiling. A few additional sets followed their gaze. With great trepidation, Christina tilted her head, not wanting to see what captured their attention, but understanding that they were trying to warn her of something. And when she saw it, she nearly choked on her bite of sandwich, coughing incessantly and drawing the attention of Robin and Jason.

The cloaked figure clung unnaturally to the foyer ceiling, staring down at them with a grimace on its alligator-skin face. It let out a deep, guttural growl and, to the horror of all three, scurried like a large cat across the ceiling towards them. Robin let out a scream, while Jason jumped from his chair, which slid loudly back into the wall. Christina backed up towards the foyer, unable to take her eyes off the creature, and felt her body crumble below her, heavy like lead. The room spun and went dark as she fell heavily to the wood floor. Jason carried her listless body to the sofa, while Robin watched in terror as the figure's mouth opened in a snarl, revealing a double set of teeth and a long, forked tongue. It crept down the wall and over the picture gallery, knocking several paintings off and leaving others tilted, before disappearing down the stairs and out of sight. Despite Robin's ability to see the dead, it was rare that she saw something as vile and evil as that creature, and it took her a few moments to catch her breath before walking over to where Jason tended to Christina.

"Is she okay?" Robin asked.

"She just fainted. Would you run over to the bathroom and grab a cold rag?"

Robin did as requested and returned a minute later.

"We don't have any more time to wait. We must leave now. Can you wake her up?" Robin asked.

Christina began to groan. "What happened? Why am I on the sofa?"

"You fainted," explained Jason.

"Oh, my head," Christina moved her hand up to her right temple, which was pink and growing swollen. "Where is it?" she jumped, suddenly remembering what transpired just prior to the fall.

Before either could answer, the sound of frenzied voices came coming from outside. Christina looked out the window, surprised to see Sam and Jeremy, tools under their arms, running through the yard. At one point, Sam dropped a hammer and did not even bother to pick it up. They were yelling frantically to each other, though it was impossible to make out what they were discussing. Jeremy looked back once before sprinting towards the tree line, Sam following closely behind. A moment later came the roar of the engine as the barge quickly escaped to the safety of the ocean. Even the rocky waters were less dangerous than Statham Island. No one had to ask what had happened. Christina knew she would probably receive a call or text message later from Jeremy, giving some excuse as to why they would be gone that afternoon…a family emergency perhaps…and she felt certain they would keep the true reason silent because they were professionals and had a reputation to maintain.

"Do you hear that?" Christina asked. It was coming from the library. The three stood up and cautiously made their way to the next room, horrified to find books flying off shelves and onto the floor. Books from high to low were cast off their wooden shelves and to the stone ground beneath them, as though the library was a toddler having a fit. One book landed on a table, teetered along the edge for a second, as if deciding whether to stay or jump, before slipping to the floor. Then, a small, gray book landed in front of Jason's feet. He picked it up and recognized the name written neatly on the front cover…Elizabeth Statham. Its leather-bound edges had long since worn, yet the unruled pages within were in optimal condition with only slight yellowing along the edges. He flipped through the book, finding a series of entries spanning the course of 1884-1885, written in a woman's fine cursive writing. The plume pen ink had dried in blots on certain pages, bleeding through and making a few of the words illegible.

"May I have it?" Robin asked. Jason handed over the book. She set the book down on one of the library tables, but before she could even sit down, the pages began to flip on their own accord, for a second resembling an open fan, before suddenly stopping on a page dated June 6, 1884:

I have spoken with George about his indecencies, yet he continues to brush me aside. He does not believe we sit at a crossroads between good and evil and is growing weary of my protests. Yet I see a change in his demeanor, one that has become hostile and concerned only with wealth. He has traded his soul for nobility and requests I do the same. But I will not disavow my Lord. George must abandon that notion, for I cannot bear the thought of cursing our family to the depths of Hell for all eternity.

The pages again flipped to another entry dated June 10, 1884:

Try as I may, he continues his ungodly antics. Our Sunday worship has been demoralized by Joshua, the man who brought this evil religion upon us. He is devoid of principles and continues to make promises that turn my God-fearing husband into one who adores the unholiest of gods.

The ceremonies took on a new disturbance Sunday when George begged my permission to offer our very son to the creature they have conjured with their evilness. And when I refused, I bound myself to joining their church in his stead. I must remove the instigator of this madness that suddenly pervades our home.

June 19, 1884:

It seems as though our new pastor has taken to inviting new guests to our chapel. George is agreeable to every whim of Joshua, and despite my pleadings with him, he perseveres. Yet these guests are not those of high society. They are vagrants and, should they never return to the mainland, would be missed by no one. I have yet to see them leave our island and am growing concerned that the mysterious dirt mounds that have appeared in our gardens as of late comprise some part of an inhumane process.

June 23, 1884:

More mysterious dirt mounds have appeared by my rose garden. Two of them, to be exact. And it is quite noteworthy that there were exactly two guests invited to Sunday mass. I cannot help but wonder whether they have become sacrifices to the false god my beloved George now serves.

The stock of Statham Oil Productions has doubled, and a slew of investors has come forth wanting to expand the company further. The past few years in such a recession have made us thirsty for the blessings of prosperity. And with each blessing, George falls further into the hands of the pastor.

I fear they have conjured something evil on our property that threatens the safety of my family. Yet, no amount of pleading with George breaks his obsession. His fear of losing his wealth, should he step away, makes him a prisoner of it.

The book flipped several months forward to December 17th:

Oh, how I enjoyed her company and talent with the children. But it seems as though our nanny, Nina, experienced an unfortunate accident on the stairs and broke her neck.

While cleaning her quarters, a maid discovered a journal hidden under her bed with information regarding George's business dealings that would have incriminated him. To think that we had a spy in our very home. A local businessman by the name of Mr. Cunningham has telegraphed, asking to know her whereabouts. We have told him that she returned to her native Ireland, and he has not telegraphed since.

The group looked at each other stunned. So the rumors swirling around the Statham's had been true. How had this diary gone unnoticed for so long, sitting amongst the collections of novels for over a century? As if in answer, Christina spotted a missing panel behind the area that several books had fallen from…a secret place that no one would have ever suspected and had allowed the diary to remain hidden all those years.

Christina felt an overwhelming feeling of fatigue and nausea overcome her and sat down in one of the library chairs, resting her head on her arms. The afternoon had taken a toll on her already weak body.

"I'll grab some water," Robin offered and walked quickly towards the kitchen. Jason sat down beside Christina. He rubbed her back, his strong hands running up and down her spine and along her shoulders. Robin returned shortly thereafter empty-handed.

"The water has turned to…blood," she said disgustedly. "Can you make it?" Christina knew she had no choice. Her legs were like rubber, and she could not even begin to stand up, much less walk to the ferry, but she would have to try.

"Jason, lift her. We can't wait any longer."

"Okay, you get the door." Jason hoisted Christina, now barely conscious, over his shoulder, and walked towards the living room. A loud crash came from behind them, and he nearly dropped her when he realized that the table on the library balcony had come crashing down onto the spot they had been sitting just seconds earlier.

"Come on!" he shouted to Robin, who herself could not believe her eyes. Up on the balcony, the cloaked figure turned away from the edge and walked back towards the upstairs hallway. She inadvertently let out a horrified scream and seemed frozen in motion as she struggled to comprehend the disastrous scene before her.

Jason grabbed her arm, pulling her out of the library, and the threesome bolted for the front door, struggling with the lock for a moment before stumbling outside. As they sprinted towards the dock, Christina opened her eyes briefly. "Oh, God! It's following us!" she yelled. Jason turned, horrified to find the creature not far behind them, moving swiftly and smoothly through the natural obstacles of the land and gaining traction quickly. They felt like bugs in a spider web, struggling forward with each step, their movements impossibly slow. And just as suddenly as it had started, the rubber band-like grip the creature had on them broke. All three fell to the ground from the sudden lack of resistance, relieved to find that the creature was no longer chasing them. But in reality, it had a more sinister plan in mind.

"Are you okay?" Jason asked, pulling Christina up.

"Yeah," she cried, mustering all of her strength to stand.

"Come on," he yelled, pulling up Robin, and the three sprinted towards the ferry, where Mike sat smoking a cigar, unaware of the plight that occurred so close by to him. Mike was surprised to find all three clamoring aboard *The Stargaze*.

"What's going on?" he asked, confused by their urgency.

"Just go!" Robin ordered. "We'll explain later."

"It may be a little bit of a rocky trip in these waters," Mike warned, though no one seemed the least bit bothered under the circumstances. "Here, take these," he said, passing around lifejackets. He started the engine and backed it away from the dock, turning it towards the mainland. The winds picked up, slapping the faces of all aboard with the sharp sting of hail that fell from the skies. Lightning flashed around them, quickly followed by a clap of thunder.

"Go, go!" Robin begged. But he seemed to have spotted something off in the distance that no one else had noticed. The others turned, following his gaze, and could see movement far off in the water…a wave that was growing quickly in size and headed in their direction.

Seconds later, it crashed against the ferry, rocking it violently and soaking all four. Another large wave hit, and then another, and Christina realized that with each impact, the ferry was being pushed back towards the Statham Island shoreline. The wind howled violently around them. The trees along the shore blew ferociously and looked as though they might snap. Any attempts to move away from the island were futile.

"It's like a hurricane!" Christina shouted, above the noise.

"We can't go anywhere until it calms down," Mike said hopelessly, pointing to the violent waters that now surrounded them. "I've never seen anything like this before. There's just no way to safely navigate through this."

There was a collective feeling of desperation. It was as though the evil of the island was holding them hostage, refusing to relinquish its grasp. Christina had the frightening realization that perhaps they would not be able to leave until it got what it wanted…new souls to add to its collection. Affirming her fears, she caught a glimpse of the cloaked figure along the tree line, blending in at times with the trees, and then reappearing in full view, taking great pleasure in their plight as it sought to orchestrate their demise.

"Look!" she pointed, gulping as she spoke. Mike stared at it for a moment and said nothing, yet his face paled, and he looked as though he was not feeling well. He began a slow navigation of the ferry out to sea, like an animal hoping to avoid detection as it escaped a predator, rough waves rocking the ferry.

He never liked storms, especially boating in them. He had seen too many accidents that left boats completely destroyed and had promised his wife that he would boat in fair weather only. She, in return, had promised to never smoke a cigarette again. It was a marital pact that they had abided by for thirty years, yet here he was, breaking his rule and wondering whether it was going to cost the group their lives in the process. But he had seen the figure for himself and knew there was no going back. This was it. Get out now, or be swallowed up by the evil that lurked on the property.

The ferry made progress, only to be hit by another wave and sent back several feet. Yet they were advancing still. A particularly strong wave crashed against the boat. By now, all aboard were completely soaked, head to toe, but this wave crash was different. It took a moment before anyone realized that what dripped from their shirts was not water, but a dark, red, viscous substance. At first, Mike worried that oil had leaked from the boat and sprayed up over them, but it was not hot like oil would have been. Another wave crashed into them, and more of the strange liquid covered them.

"My God, it's blood!" Robin yelled.

"Where is it coming from?" Jason asked.

All four looked out at the water and realized they were surrounded by a dark, crimson sea that splashed along the white ferry, leaving splatter marks behind, reminiscent of a murder scene. The hail had given way to heavy rains, which made clear streaks down the red substance, only to vanish beneath redness with the next wave. They huddled together under the small, covered portion of the ferry. Bloody water collected around them in the uncovered sections faster than it could drain out, and there was a common fear among all of them that the boat would begin to list to one side or, even worse, capsize.

Mike did his best to distance the ferry from the island, yet after half an hour, was only twenty feet offshore. The Stargaze was a strong, yet small, ferry that was not designed to withstand violent weather. With his focus dedicated to dodging stray waves that might capsize the vessel, it was nearly impossible to make headway. And he knew that their danger would only increase once they entered deeper water.

"It's useless," he admitted to the surprise of all around him. "It's not letting up. We are going to get hurt if we stay out in this."

"We can't go back!" Christina found herself yelling angrily.

"We may have no choice."

"It's now or never," she yelled back. "If we don't make it out right now, we may as well just jump into the ocean and be swept away." Her eyes looked tired and her body weak, and despite the life jacket, he doubted she had the strength to survive the sheer weight of the waves hitting her.

"Mike needs to head two hundred yards west. The waves are calmer, and he will be able to sail north to the mainland from there," Jason said in a low voice to Christina. His experience in the rough Alaskan waters as a child was coming in handy.

"Jason thinks we should head west two hundred yards, and then we'd be safe to go north," Christina relayed. She wondered why she was relaying the message when the two men were only an arm's length apart from each other. Mike looked at her with an odd expression, perhaps sharing her thoughts, before turning his attention west. After a minute of consideration, he began to navigate in that direction without saying a word. She glanced at Jason, who was quietly sitting by himself, appearing distracted. She sat down beside him and asked whether he was okay.

"Yeah, I just feel a little off. I'm going to step outside for some fresh air."

"Do you want me to come with you?"

"No, you stay here. I love you." Jason stood up and walked out of the covered section while Robin and Christina watched Mike's unwavering focus on the sea before him.

"Love you too," Christina called after him.

The ferry continued to travel west and eventually made it past the far edge of Statham Island. Christina breathed a sigh of relief when they, at last, reached open waters and began to head north towards the mainland and was joined by Robin and Mike in her reprieve. Jason had been right about the boat course. She left the covered area, eager to congratulate him on his nautical prowess, but found only empty benches. She called his name and briskly walked the ferry perimeter, but Jason was nowhere to be found.

"Where's Jason?" she asked frantically as she re-entered the room. "Oh my God, where is he?" she panicked. She was met with silence, and there was only one viable explanation that came to mind. "He's fallen overboard! We have to go back!" she yelled. Robin and Mike did not move. "I said we have to go back!" she repeated, growing angry at their lack of urgency. Why weren't they responding? "Mike! Robin! Did you not hear me? Jason fell overboard!"

Robin finally responded calmly, "Sit down for a minute."

"Sit down? There's no time for that. We need to go back." Growing more frantic, she took control of the steering wheel from Mike. She did not know how to operate the ferry but was going to find out, with or without his help.

"Stop, just stop," Mike intervened. "You need to talk to Robin."

"What's going on here? Don't you care?" She turned the boat around and began to head back before Mike pulled the keys from the ignition, and the ferry came to a gradual stop. They were several minutes off the Statham Island shoreline, nearly half the way to the mainland, and the only motion came from the light rocking of waves that playfully pushed against the ferry from time to time. The waves had returned to a grayish, clear hue and had washed away most of the blood from the ferry.

"There is something I need to tell you," Robin said, holding Christina close and leading her over to a seat. She wrapped damp blankets over Christina's shoulders and her own. "Just calm down. Jason did not fall overboard."

"Then where is he?" Christina asked between gritted teeth, struggling to not shout.

"There was an accident a few weeks ago, a horrible accident. Don't you remember?"

"What accident? The greenhouse?"

"No, dear. I'm talking about the *other* accident."

Christina shook her head in confusion.

Robin went on, "Jason told me that it was the day after he first kissed you." There was sadness in her eyes as she talked.

Christina just looked at her with a blank stare. She vividly remembered the day they had visited a museum and an assortment of little shops in East Hampton and shared their first kiss after a romantic bike ride. She shuddered when she recalled how the day ended as they discovered a trespasser upon their return home. It had been several weeks, and the following day was somewhat of a blur, but deciphering the disturbing message on the book stack came to mind. That's right, and she had looked for Jason to tell him about the message that read, *Leave before it's too late. Get out!* She recalled Sam telling her that Jason was outside taking care of Ralphie.

A look of distress overcame her. "Oh, no!" Something horrible had happened, but she struggled to remember what.

Robin looked at her compassionately. "Do you remember now, honey?"

"I…I don't know. I remember something. I went outside to find Jason…I needed to talk to him...and then I found him holding the little puppy who lived with us at the time. Only he wasn't holding the puppy. The puppy was there, but it was still in its playpen, digging away at the ground. I went back to the manor to look for him there but stopped when I saw something in the shrubbery." She stopped for a moment, tears in her eyes. "It was Jason." Robin held her close, as Christina let out a loud wail, the type of sound reserved for learning the news of a loved one's death.

"I know it's hard," Robin said apologetically.

"He must have gone up to fix something on the roof and just slipped." Her mind returned to the moment she saw the lifelessness in his eyes and realized he was gone. But just as quickly, she was brought back into a reality in which he was very much alive and present in her life. She felt a wave of anger come over her as she struggled to discern what was real and what was not. She fidgeted with her engagement ring, twisting it around her finger anxiously. Only, it was not the pear-shaped ring Jason proposed with. This ring held a center diamond surrounded by rubies…her grandmother's. She had kept the ring locked away in the safe, given her fear of losing stones during renovation projects, and did not remember putting it on.

"But how could it be?" she protested. "I've spent every day with him. He lives with me. You saw him yourself tonight. And Mike, too." The more she talked, the angrier she felt. Was Robin simply too fearful of the island to return to look for him? Was she that frightened that she would abandon a person in need of help?

"I'm sorry to have to be the one to tell you, dear, but Jason passed away that day. It is his spirit you've been seeing and communicating with. Just as I'm psychic and can interact with those who have died, so can you. We share that ability. You just have not yet learned how to discern the living from the dead, but I can teach you.”

“What do you mean? I’ve been living with a spirit this whole time? That makes no sense.”

“Some things cannot be explained. There is a lot we do not understand about the spirit world.”

“Well, what about Mike? Mike saw Jason, too. And his brother and another crew member have worked with him at the manor every day and never once discussed his death with me.”

“Mike has the ability to sense spirits. He cannot see or communicate with them. You may have noticed the two did not talk during our visit. The rumor around town is that the other two men working on the property have simply been too distraught to talk about Jason’s death to anyone, even their own families, so it is likely they did not want to talk about it with you. Perhaps it would have made finishing an already difficult project that much harder.”

Christina thought back to Jason and Mike’s interactions. Robin was right. She could not recall any conversations they had had as of late. She had also found it odd that Mike never returned the wave or nod Jason often gave in greeting. The thought crossed her mind that perhaps this would also explain the distanced relationship she had noticed between Jason and the other crew members.

“If Jason is dead, does he know?” It was a valid question. It made her sad to think that he could be stuck in limbo. “And why did you wait to tell me until now?”

“We spoke, and he understands now. He tried to stay with you as long as he could tonight to protect you, but his spirit could not leave the island. For the moment, at least, he is attached to the place he perished. But I expect that very soon, he will move on. The creature no longer has control of the spirits of Statham Island, and they are free to cross over when they are ready. I would have told you sooner, but there was no chance. We were under attack."

"What about Bob? Is he okay?"

"Yes, we spoke when I did my walk-around of the island, and he actually crossed over just before we left. I have missed him dearly, but it brought me so much peace to help him one last time, so thank you. You know, he is the one who left you that message with the books, and he has been protecting you as well."

The ferry neared the shoreline, the freak storm having dissipated and the waves now calm. Lightning flashed in the direction of Statham Island, as if a storm cloud hung perpetually above the land, ready to snuff out any chance of light.

Donna, the Volvo, sat waiting just where Christina had parked it, a ticket now on the windshield for a parking violation. Evidently, she had parked in the spot longer than the month she had pre-purchased. She tore up the ticket and tossed it into the ocean. Nothing mattered anymore.

Soaked and tired, Robin drove Christina to her house, allowing her to stay in her guest room for as long as she needed. Donna would have to stay put for at least another day. It felt great to don dry clothes and lay in the queen guest bed, filled with oversized pillows and soft sheets. The bed felt like a hammock, holding her like a child in a mother's embrace, yet she tossed and turned the entire night, waking up several times, mourning the loss of Jason and longing to be with him.

Chapter Thirteen

Robin awoke early the next morning. She prepared a full breakfast of eggs, bacon, and toast, along with coffee and juice. A desire to help Christina get back on her feet had grown within her, and she was prepared for her to stay in the guest room for as long as needed. She set the breakfast table, complete with flowers in the center, excited to have a guest in her home and wanting to make a good impression. She sat for half an hour, then forty-five minutes, before getting up to knock on Christina's door. She had not wanted to wake her up but also did not want the food to go bad. No one answered. She knocked again.

"Christina, breakfast is ready, dear." Still no response. "Christina?" She turned the knob, expecting to perhaps encounter her walking out of the bathroom, but when the door opened, there was only an empty room. The bed was neatly made, and a note sat by its edge.

Dear Robin,

Words cannot thank you enough for your kindness and generosity when I needed it most. For that, I will always be grateful. But I cannot stay. I have returned to Statham Manor. It is where I belong now and where Jason awaits. Without him, I am lost. It is more than that, though. The manor needs someone to care for it…to love it. It needs me like a child, their mother. It is mine, and I am its. Please do not come after me. It is a decision I have made after much consideration, and by the time you read this, I will have likely already returned.

Should we meet again, I hope that it is under different circumstances. Until then, take care of yourself.

Christina

The color rushed from her face. She knew that it was highly unlikely she would be able to escape the island a second time. There was only one other ferry in the area besides Mike's, and it departed at nine o'clock for various stops around East Hampton. If it was not a busy day, Christina could certainly pay the operator to take her the short distance to Statham Island. She had only twelve minutes to make it before it left. Grabbing her keys, she ran out the door and jumped into her car. Halfway there, she came upon an accident. A car had run a stop sign, hitting another car in its path, causing the road to close temporarily. She knew the back roads well and took the quickest detour possible towards the dock, arriving with three minutes to spare. There was an audible sigh of relief when she saw that the ferry was still docked. An older couple sat on the ferry's benches, but Christina was nowhere to be found. Robin wondered whether she had, by the grace of God, changed her mind at the last minute. She ran over to the middle-aged man standing by the ferry and asked if he had seen a woman fitting Christina's description.

"Oh, yeah. I saw her about an hour ago, down here by the pier. I asked her if she was okay. Her hair was messy and her clothes dirty, and these days, you never know if someone is on drugs or whatnot."

"Where did she go?" she asked, desperately scanning the growing number of passengers traversing the parking lot.

"I gave her a ride over to Statham Island. You know, that little island over…"

"I know what it is, that evil place," Robin groaned. "You gave her a ride *there*?"

He looked puzzled by her comment. "Yeah, well, that's where she asked to go. She's lucky I got here early this morning. It's about to get busy shuttling folks here and there with the weekend around the corner."

"Thanks for your help," she said, giving a half wave as she walked away.

Robin called Mike and told him what had happened. The two discussed whether or not to travel back out to the island and decided against it, at least for the moment and until Christina was ready to leave for good. They could not risk the danger they experienced the night before.

Meanwhile, Christina sat on the pier that the ferry had dropped her off at thirty minutes prior, somewhat hesitant to approach the manor. She did not regret her decision to return but feared what she would find inside, alone, after having been gone for an evening.

She had left Robin's house before anyone would notice, afraid she would be talked out of returning to the island, and had taken a taxi to the dock. She wondered whether Robin had discovered her absence yet. If she had not, she would very soon. A sense of guilt suddenly made its way into her conscience.

Christina finally mustered the courage to walk the short distance to the front door. The manor beckoned her, as if reaching out with welcoming arms and reeling her in. The sheer magnificence with which it presented itself captivated her. There was an unwavering fascination with the building that, for a moment, caught her off guard, as if seeing it for the first time, and drowned out everything else around her. The home bragged of a grandeur that one could not find in any modern-day house, one that was relegated to the homes of generations past. The familiar faces in the dining room oil paintings, all hanging in their original spots, greeted her with curious eyes, as if wondering where she had been. Christina stood for a second, staring back into their eyes, wondering what they had been up to while she was gone. The sound of classical music startled her back into reality and came from the grand living room, as if being played on an old gramophone. There was no such instrument present, yet the sound radiated smoothly and splendidly through the rooms, seeming at times to come from all directions. The manor had missed her and was apologizing in some way, she thought to herself. She was home.

"Jason," she called, yet no one responded. "Jason," she called again, making her way to the attic. "I'm home." She ran her hand along the woodwork of the stairwell as she walked up, stopping every few steps to examine the relief carvings in greater detail. Upon reaching the top floor, she was flabbergasted to find that the attic suite had taken on a new sense of charm, as if it had been expecting her. The bed was neatly made with a tray and flowers sitting atop. The furniture was dusted. Even the curtains looked to have been washed and ironed. She looked down at the kitchen table to find a warm cup of coffee waiting for her, and when she turned, Jason was standing in the doorway. The sound of the music downstairs was loud enough to hear, even in the attic.

"Is it true?" Christina asked. "Are you…?" But she couldn't even finish her question. He was there before her, his smile and strong arms just as she remembered.

He took her hand, and the two began to dance, slowly, closely, and she could swear she could feel the beat of his heart tapping next to hers. She glanced down to find the pear-shaped engagement ring back on her finger where it belonged. It was as though everything was as though it should be.

"I want to show you something," Jason said, pulling Christina after him as he excitedly moved towards the doorway with a childlike enthusiasm.

"Okay, where are we going?" Christina asked, excitedly.

"You'll see." Jason sometimes had the habit of biting his lip when he was particularly excited about something, and when he spoke again, Christina could see a tooth mark fade from his bottom lip. "Over here." He walked towards the taxidermy room, unlocking it with a key off of the master key ring. The room was dank, dark, and devoid of life except for the remnants of animals from another era. "This way," he said, motioning for her to follow.

"It's dark. Turn on the light." Christina did not like the room, particularly when she could not see the darkest corners. Ever since the tour of the manor with Annette, she had avoided it and only entered when absolutely necessary.

"Just trust me," Jason begged. Christina did as he asked and held his hand, following his lead through. Then suddenly, there was light. A door on the far side of the room opened before them, seemingly of its own accord. Up until that point, she had been unaware that the room even had a second door. Her curiosity grew stronger still when she saw what was on the other side…a small, frail-looking balcony, overlooking the rose gardens along the east side of the property. At one time, it must have been quite attractive, with its white, Italianesque balusters and perhaps a small table and chairs for enjoying the views, but what remained were the chippy remains of a structure that should have been removed during renovations. She wondered how, after all this time working day in and day out on the property, it could possibly have gone unnoticed.

Under normal conditions, she would have avoided such a balcony for fear of falling through, but Jason assured her it was stable and she had nothing to worry about. He offered a hand to Christina as she cautiously stepped out and into his arms. As the two stood, observing the beauty of the gardens and the ocean beyond, she felt her right foot sink into one of the wood boards beneath, its softness no longer capable of supporting weight. She grabbed ahold of the wooden railing for balance, half expecting it to snap apart in her grasp like the railing at the far end, which sat broken, its pieces scattered about the balcony. There was relief when it did not come crashing down, taking her along with it, but also fear that the next misstep might. She proceeded warily, holding Jason's hand tightly.

"What is this?" she asked nervously, looking to the ground below and then quickly away. She had always been fearful of heights.

"I found it while fixing the roof but wanted to wait until the right time to show you." Jason seemed genuinely proud of the find.

But a horrible realization came over Christina. Had this been where Jason fell? And if so, why would he bring her to such a dangerous spot? Instinctively, her feet shifted in the direction of the door.

"It seems like it's about to collapse. We should go back," she said, turning to step back inside. But just as she was about to enter the taxidermy room, the door slammed shut before her with a loud bang that shook the balcony, causing a few more balusters to break loose. She pushed the door, trying to force it open, but it was locked from the inside. She pushed again, hoping that the heavy door would miraculously budge, but it remained fixed, as if glued shut. "Jason, it's stuck!" she yelled frantically, at the same time kicking herself for having done something so stupid. There was no other way off the balcony. The roof was too steep to walk on, and she would surely fall three stories if she tried. She could see a window six feet over. If she could just stretch…maybe carefully jump…from the balcony's edge, she could reach it, yet it would do no good if it was locked.

She turned to Jason, feeling betrayed. "Why did you bring me out here?" But the man before her was no longer the one she had fallen in love with. His plaid shirt and jeans had been replaced by an all-too-recognizable cloak that she had grown to dread…his kind face, now primitive, animalistic, its reptilian-like skin a warning of danger to others. Red, piercing eyes stared at her in anger. The creature let out a deep, guttural laugh that seemed to bounce off the walls of the manor in a horrifying echo, shaking the balcony and sending shivers down her spine and paralyzing her in fear.

The realization that it meant to kill her sent Christina into a state of fight-or-flight. There was nowhere to go except down. She was trapped. And so her only option became to fight that which had tormented her for so long.

A loose baluster hung from what remained of the railing, threatening to fall with the slightest breeze, and easily popped off with a firm yank. The narrow neck provided an ideal spot to hold, just small enough to fit within the grasp of her hand. But a swift swing at the creature hit only air. Christina quickly swung again at its arm, this time causing it to momentarily wince in pain. But the hit only served to anger the creature, who charged towards her. She ducked out of the way of its path and swung once more, this time hitting its abdomen. An enraged growl followed as it swiped her backside with its long claws, leaving a set of deep, crimson marks. Christina let out a scream as she writhed in pain. It struck again, leaving a second set of claw marks. Blood soaked through her shirt, its white now drenched in red. She was just about to forfeit, to surrender herself to a force that seemed infinitely stronger than her, but mustering the courage to swing once more, she hit it hard in the chest. It winced in pain and let out a horrendous growl.

"You cannot escape!" it taunted.

The creature prepared to retaliate. Gathering all of her courage, she yelled, "This is not your home. You are not welcome here. Get out!" And as she yelled, all of the pain that the island had caused was released. The creature stopped, appearing wounded. "Get out!" she repeated!" It took a step back, hunched over.

She felt the floor beneath her shake, as if emanating the creature's anger. The railing and balusters separated from the balcony and dangled over the large drop off for a second before hitting the edge of the roof and making a final descent to the bushes below. The creature angrily grabbed her, and she felt herself go limp, as though she were an insect caught in a spider's web and had just had the juice sucked out of her. The last thing she remembered was praying for protection.

It was a familiar voice that brought her back into consciousness. "Christina, honey, wake up. It's gone now." She awoke to find Jason over her, his pale, blue eyes staring down into hers. Christina jumped back, unsure whether she could trust the man before her. "It's me. Don't be afraid." He reached out, pulling her up and out of the way, just in time to avoid the creature's charge towards her that almost surely would have sent her flying over the edge of the balcony. They watched from the doorway, horrified, as it tumbled over the edge, disappearing from their lives forever. It was gone.

A loud, squeaky sound resonated, and a few floorboards fell off the balcony, followed by the sole lingering railing. The remainder of the balcony separated from the manor and followed the rest of the debris to the ground. Christina breathed a sigh of relief and hugged Jason, a little hesitantly at first, and remained in his embrace for some time.

The two strolled to the beach, making the walk that they had taken so many times before. Once again, the island resumed a welcoming atmosphere. The sun shone a little brighter. The birds chirped a little louder. She hoped it would remain and that the evil of the island was banished forever this time.

The ocean waves softly tapped the shore, and a few sailboats could be seen far off in the distance, enjoying the last of the good sailing weather of the year. The white sands were filled with new shells, evidence that nature carries on in spite of hardship and death. Soon, the cold would set in. The sea life would move to deeper waters, and not so long from now, the sands would be covered in snow. Christina was reminded that just as nature's continual rebirth allows it to stay healthy and thrive, so too does a rebirth of the human spirit from time to time. And despite their struggles along the way, Statham Island and Christina had both given each other a fresh start.

Jason looked tired. His coloring was pale, his blue eyes nearly colorless. It looked as though he was fading away before her. "I can't stay," Jason finally said. "I'm sorry. It's my time to go."

Christina pleaded with him to stay. "Please don't go. Don't leave me here alone."

He stroked her cheek. "Know that when the leaves blow on a cool Fall morning, that is me whispering 'I love you.' When the warm sunshine hits your body, that is me hugging you. And when a bird sits by your window, chirping a sweet melody, that is me singing to you. I'll always love you." His frame began to match the ocean in the distance as he faded away, out of the grasp of her hands, and she could feel in her soul that his spirit had left.

"I'll always love you too," she whispered into emptiness. For the first time, she made the walk back to the manor alone, mourning Jason's loss while simultaneously celebrating that he had found peace.

For a while, the house took on what can only be described as a normal character. The lights shone brightly from the light fixtures. Sunlight poured through the windows, the invisible veil of occlusion gone. The oil paintings in the gallery maintained their original forms, no longer deviating in response to the surrounding environment, though a new one had mysteriously found its place amongst the collection…this one of a man, sitting alone on the beach, staring out at the water. He had a peaceful smile, as if all was right in the world. The horrendous, rotten smell of the chapel was replaced by the scent of fresh roses, and for the first time, light shone brightly through the stained glass Jesus and sheep, casting a vibrant rainbow of colors along the floor and walls. Christina no longer heard voices or saw visions of the wanderers, as she had come to call the lost spirits of the island, and the dreams of the creature that had haunted her for months came to an abrupt end. But she feared the calm on the island was likely temporary, just as it had been before, and decided to leave the following day after Annette's visit.

The next morning, she awoke early. The leaves outside had become a blur of yellows, oranges, and reds, and when the wind blew, reminded Christina of a campfire. For the first time in a while, she was longing to see Charlie and Chelsea and promised herself that she would take them camping before the cold set in. Her luggage was packed, and she had just made herself a cup of coffee when she heard a loud knock coming from the front door. Still in her robe, she ran down to the foyer, surprised to find that Annette had arrived so early. Excitedly, she flung open the door and hugged her friend, as if she had not seen her in years.

"Wow, you need company more often," Annette joked.

"I just made some coffee. Want a cup?"

"I'd love some," she said. "This place looks amazing. I mean, look at the walls. The wallpaper was falling off, and the floors were so damaged, and now it looks like a magazine cover," she said, admiring the dining room. They walked the manor and the property, and Annette oohed and awed at the perfection and attention to detail with which the renovations had been completed.

"Are you ready to get back to real life?" Annette asked. "Did you miss the hustle and bustle of the city?"

"I think I'm ready." She handed the keys back to Annette and closed the large double doors to the manor for the last time. That chapter of her life was over and done with.

Mike stood waiting by The Stargaze Express and gave Christina a nod. He thought she was crazy for returning to the island but was relieved to see that she had decided to leave it behind for good. The two discussed nothing of the other night. Maybe one day, they would meet at a restaurant and talk about what happened, but neither wanted to discuss it in front of Annette. The events would sound too unbelievable to an outsider, and it was easier to keep it a secret for the moment.

Despite his fear of the island, Mike carried all of the luggage and final renovation debris to the ferry. Sam and Jeremy had not bothered to return, choosing to risk a possible ding to their reputation over setting foot on the island again, leaving Christina with the few remaining bags of garbage. As the three made a final walk to the dock, Christina could hear the wind pick up. A fresh red leaf fell onto her sweater, and she put it in her purse. She would come to collect these little signs of Jason in a scrapbook, eventually filling it with items that told a love story better than a collection of love letters. Every so often, when the pain of missing Jason seemed too great, Christina would hear a cardinal sing on her windowsill and know the melody was meant for her.

Not long after, Christina moved into the new three-bedroom Manhattan apartment. John reluctantly let Charlie and Chelsea join and only relented at the request of Rachel, who, now seven months pregnant, became more vocal in wanting the house to be for their "new" family. John resumed his minimalist parenting, taking the children every other weekend, but only after first checking with his wife, who often requested that a weekend be skipped in lieu of their social plans. Once the baby arrived, she became the center of their world, and the twins took a back seat.

Christina went on to work as a solo practitioner, opening her own practice in order to have more flexibility and, ultimately, more time with the children. A week after moving in, she also received a new social security card. She was no longer Christina Martin in the eyes of the state. She was now Christina Taylor, just as she had been prior to her marriage. She felt free for the first time in years; free of the heartbreak that followed her divorce, free to be the best in her field without the expectations of a large firm, free to be the mother she had always longed to become, and free from the evil of Statham Island.

From time to time, she would experience premonitions through dreams or find that she could see and interact with those that others did not notice. Robin helped her to build upon her abilities, and the two women would eventually team up to help numerous others dealing with the paranormal. Chelsea shared this special gift and would one day find that her abilities far exceeded either of theirs.

After the initial sale of Statham Island fell through, Annette immediately re-listed the estate with her realtor. Her greatest fear was the languishing of the property on the market and a potential depreciation with weather-related wear and tear. Despite the unfavorable reputation of the island amongst locals, it gained positive attention from ads placed within the larger cities of New York, New Jersey, Connecticut, and Rhode Island:

Do not miss out on this once-in-a-lifetime opportunity to purchase your own island, located just off the East Hampton coast. Twenty-two acres of land with mature forestry offer walking trails, private beach access, and beautiful gardens. A recently renovated manor with twelve bedrooms and nine bathrooms provides an

A young couple, Drs. Andrew and Olivia Thompson of New Haven, looking to leave their positions at Yale University behind, purchased the island the following spring. According to their marriage counselor, the stress and time commitment of teaching and doing research had forged a hole in their relationship that required them to take a step back from their busy lives to heal. The island would serve as their refuge from the modern world. Although the two professors had stashed away a small fortune, they hoped to continue to earn a living, just in a way that would allow them to spend more time together and rebuild their marriage.

Andrew had come up with the idea of opening a workplace retreat, rentable by individual companies, for their employees to complete training activities and team-building exercises. He felt confident that his business background could quickly make the island profitable and that all of the funds they had put into purchasing the property would be quickly regained.

Olivia shared her husband's enthusiasm, and once she visited the property, found herself very much drawn in. As soon as the papers were signed, she hurriedly began to make purchases to transform the stately manor into a resort. Despite the immense work done by Christina and the renovation crew, the pool on the property had evidently been ignored. Sam and Jeremy's rapid departure had been quickly followed by a cancellation by the pool company hired by Annette to clean it, so its pond-like appearance prevailed. Olivia purchased a collection of lounges, tables and chairs, and umbrellas for the pool area and then drained the water and scrubbed the walls and floor herself. The cleaned pool, with its furnished decking, now looked inviting and party-ready.

She continued to make her way around the property, purchasing wicker, cushioned sofas, and potted faux greenery, requiring minimal upkeep, for the patio behind the manor. Soon after, concrete benches flanked the fountain at the front of the manor. The cigar room became a sauna, and the sunroom a spa. The large dining room table was replaced by smaller tables to better accommodate several groups of people at a time.

The business did well. Every large corporation along the East Coast wanted to rent out the facility, and within two months, it had been booked out through the following year. The companies and their employees loved it, and the Thompsons contemplated never returning to academia. There was no reason to ever go back. They were happier and closer working on the island than they had been at any point in their marriage, and the prospect of starting a family became a topic of private conversation.

One morning, Andrew was in the living room, enjoying his coffee while reading the newspaper. A group was expected that evening, and there was nearly an entire day that he and Olivia would have to relax before they arrived. A knock came from the front door. He looked at his watch and, somewhat confused, walked over to the door. Olivia met him in the foyer.

"Did they change their plans? I thought they weren't coming until this evening," Andrew said.

"I thought so, too," Olivia responded, equally confused. "I haven't finished getting the rooms ready."

The knock came again, louder, and they wondered whether the knocker had overheard them.

"Who is it?" called out Andrew. Growing up in a large city, he instinctively was nervous about answering the door for anyone unexpected. No one answered, and the question was repeated. He looked at Olivia and whispered for her to bring him his Smith and Wesson. She left as requested, and he cracked open the door. Much to his surprise, there was no one there. He stepped out and looked around the vast, open landscape, and still no one. But as he turned to go back inside, a forceful gust of wind blew the double doors wide open, nearly knocking him to the floor. He got up, stunned, and quickly closed the doors.

"What is it? What happened?" asked Olivia, dutifully carrying his weapon over.

"I don't know," Andrew replied. "There was a burst of wind that just knocked me over."

"Was anyone there?"

"No, no one," he said, puzzled.

The couple just brushed the incident aside, assuming the strong wind had perhaps caused a branch to hit the home in such a way that it sounded like knocking and continued on as normal. Later in the day, the guests arrived as planned, all excited to be visiting the island for the second time. They planned to stay for two nights and had flown in from Atlanta to a smaller airport nearby. But that evening, everything changed.

A woman in the group ran down the stairs in the middle of the night, hysterical, stating that she could not sleep in the house. Olivia tried to comfort her, but she was inconsolable. She shook as she described having seen a dark, cloaked figure walking through her bedroom and absolutely refused to go back into the room. Mike's ferry picked the woman up early the next morning. She did not even wait for breakfast and sat outside with her luggage for forty-five minutes, waiting for the ferry to arrive.

The next evening, a group of young men from the same group scampered down the stairs. They claimed to have seen a strange figure roaming the hallway between their bedrooms. One gentleman even said that the figure stopped to look at him and growled to get out. After this incident, the rest of the group was on edge and, like the woman the night before, eagerly left first thing the following morning. Andrew and Olivia were stunned and could come up with no reasonable explanation for what happened.

Life at the manor quickly deteriorated from there. Every single group thereafter had some incident involving a sighting of a cloaked figure, movement of furniture on its own accord, or the disappearance of personal items. Suddenly, the reservations started to dry up. Word was spreading about the manor quickly, and no one wanted to stay there.

The Thompsons were left with no choice but to give up their dreams for the island and return to academia. And just like that, the property was once again listed for sale. Yet this time, rumors about the island had ruined its reputation far beyond the locals. A reporter wrote an article entitled, *Island from Hell*, which described the sordid history of the property and its links to the occult. From that point on, the only interest in the island came from those seeking a ghostly experience. Looting and vandalism soon overtook the property as mischievous youngsters and thrill seekers descended on the deserted island. They found their way, often by renting or stealing watercrafts, and would sometimes stay for weeks at a time. Every now and then, they never left, and their bodies were discovered only once a missing person's report was filed by concerned friends and family. And in a vicious cycle, the manor once again fell into disrepair.

Statham Island languished on the market, and the longer it sat, the more it decreased in value until, eventually, the Thompsons relinquished the property to the bank, giving up their life savings in favor of cutting all ties to the land. To this day, the island sits abandoned, shrouded in mystery, continuing to lure in the vulnerable and naïve. Some might say that the island merely waits and bides its time until it can collect more victims and that the evil that resides there has no intention of leaving. Perhaps they are right. Only time will tell.

Author's bio:

Anita Giannantonio is a Pennsylvania-based horror novelist whose passion for spine-chilling stories began with a lifelong fascination with horror films and books, further fueled by her own paranormal encounters. Her novels masterfully dive into the timeless battle between good and evil, gripping readers with tension and eerie suspense. Notably, each of her novels is crafted with precisely thirteen chapters—a nod to the superstition that led hotels and apartment buildings to omit the thirteenth floor. Anita is also the author of Insane and is currently at work on her third novel. She lives with her husband and their five children, finding inspiration in both family life and the mysteries lurking beyond the ordinary.